Ghosted by Love

KATHRYN COVENS

Cover Design & Tagline: Mary Dublin @bookcoversbydublin

Published by: Feeling Through Fiction House

ISBN: 979-8-9901649-2-5 (paperback)

Contents

For Stephanie,
may every Howl find their Calcifer.

Note from the Author

Ghosted by Love is a semi-cozy paranormal romance that contains content some readers may find disturbing. If you do not wish to receive these warnings ahead of time, please feel free to skip the next paragraph and dive into reading.

This story has references of: abduction, blood, bullying, misogyny, physical altercations, stalking.

If after reading this book you believe something should be added to this list, please reach out to the author's team at kathryncovens@gmail.com.

CHAPTER 1

Willow

I was twenty when I realized the life I saw for myself didn't exist.

Jarring, isn't it? To figure out the future you saw inside your head is nothing but a fairytale outside of it. It certainly was for me. It'd taken me close to a year to figure out where I could go to start over. When I finally found my new home, the last thing I expected was to be sharing it with the resident ghost. I certainly hadn't predicted that same ghost would become one of the most important people–well, beings–in my life. It was concerning the amount of times I caught myself thinking about him instead of paying attention to the things around me. Things like one of my favorite wolf shifters recounting her latest dating disaster.

"So I'm sitting there, eating my chicken katsu, and the man casually mentions he's still married. He just continued right along with the rest of his story as if he hadn't just dropped half the ceiling on my head like it was a fleck of dust," Arya continued after taking a hefty gulp of pinot noir. "I kid you not, Willow, he just slipped it in right between talking about the puppy eating the throw pillows and his roommates—his six, grown *adult* roommates—all figuring out their various stages of dysfunctional relationships. Oh, and did I mention one of his roommates is his wife? Yeah. He lives with the wife he didn't mention having along with five other friends."

"Where did you find this guy?" I asked, shaking my head and grabbing another glass to dry as I leaned behind the bar. We didn't open for another twenty minutes, but I let her in early to start drowning her woes while I set up.

Arya was one of the first people I met when I came to the Sun Meadow Pack. Starting over and settling down somewhere, especially after a year of wandering from pack to pack was more than a little nerve-wracking. I'd gone to the bar my first night in town to get a feel for the locals before deciding if I'd stay for a few days or continue passing through. Arya had walked straight up to me, taken the stool next to mine, and demanded I do a shot with her in feminine solidarity after the awful day she'd had. After I got over the initial shock I agreed, gag reflex and nasty alcohol choices be damned. I remembered very little of the rest of that night, but I'd woken up next to her on Beck's bathroom floor the next day.

We'd been inseparable ever since.

"The burlesque club in the city—you know, the one we went to for Megan's bachelorette party," she huffed, "I should've known he was too good to be true when he was willing to drive all the way down here for dinner. He was too considerate. I can't believe I was going to make him my Valentine. I guess it'll be another holiday alone in the books for me."

She tipped her head back and downed the rest of her glass before slamming both it and her head on the bar.

"You break that glass," I warned, "and you get to tell Beckett, and he's already annoyed with you about the chandelier."

The bar owner, and the Alpha of our pack, was generally a patient man, but Arya had a special talent for pushing those talents to their limit. A skill which she seemed to take great pleasure in at times.

"You let me worry about Beck. Plus, I said I was sorry!" She mumbled into the wood, "But really, how was I supposed to know it was so flimsy?"

"Breaking under the weight of a two hundred and twenty pound man doesn't make it flimsy. I don't know what you were thinking, making that dare." I shook my head and sliced the last lemon, turning to store the container in the mini fridge under the bar, "You're lucky no one got hurt and Beck didn't ban you for life."

"Agree to disagree," Arya sighed and looked up at me, resting her chin on the bar in place of her forehead and pursing her heart-shaped lips in a pout, "Make me a vodka cranberry next?"

"Are you sure that's a good idea? That was your second glass. Aren't you volunteering at the animal shelter tomorrow?"

"I'm sure," she nodded, "I don't have to be there until

two which gives me plenty of time to wake up at ten, lie in bed for thirty minutes contemplating if this is how I die, then crawl in the shower and promise myself I'll never drink again. After that, I'll get dressed, scarf down a gallon of coffee and a box of mac and cheese, then be on my merry way with ten minutes to spare. We both know I'd never leave the animals or the shelter staff in the lurch. Make the drink."

I made the drink.

Clearing away her empty glass and replacing it with the new concoction, I left her to her own musings and continued my routine by wiping down the rest of the butcher block bar top. There was peace in it, the mindless muscle memory that I'd gained from the seven years working at Howl. Serving drinks and waiting tables in a small town pack was the polar opposite of what I'd always planned to do —of what I'd done—and yet, I couldn't be more grateful to be doing it.

I'd come to the Sun Meadow Pack looking for a place to rebuild with nothing: no connections, no place to live, and no idea if starting over was the smartest or dumbest thing I'd ever done. It'd been impulsive, really, choosing to stay, but something about this town and these people made it feel right. It was primarily made of wolf shifters, so I fit right in, but there was so much more to it than just existing with other wolves.

I'd left my last pack without a destination in mind. I just drove and drove—praying to whatever entity who may be listening that somewhere 'far enough away' even existed. It wasn't just the desperation to escape that pushed me to keep going, it was the pursuit of something I didn't realize I'd been missing—peace.

"Five minutes till we open!" Red, our surly head cook, shouted in the kitchen before hollering only a fraction more quietly, "Five minutes and you're just arriving?"

My guess was Danny, the newest line cook had come through the back door. He was late, but that was cause for neither concern nor surprise based on the past two weeks he'd been working with us.

"S-Sorry, Red," he stammered, "I'll start chopping the veggies."

"Damn straight, you will. Honestly, you kids these days just—" I tuned out whatever rant Red delved into as I finished rolling a final set of silverware in the maroon cloth napkins before taking a tub full out on the floor to set the tables. Red was always ranting about something or other. By now his cursing and grumbling was akin to elevator music in my ears.

"Evening, Willow!" Came Paisley's chipper voice as she exited the back hallway, "Ready for a great night?"

She had what many would call a megawatt smile that regularly donned her angelic face. With her golden hair, bright blue eyes, and constant cheerfulness, I was convinced she'd been a sun deity in a past life.

"Let's hope so." It was either going to be a great night, or a rowdy one. Red mentioned seeing what he thought was a bachelor party from out of town staying at the inn down the road. We were the only bar within walking distance which could mean one of two things: a big tip or a big headache.

Sometimes both, but the tip never seemed to be worth the headache.

I walked back to grab my little apron from under the bar and tied it through the belt loops of my jeans while I walked to unlock the front doors. No doubt, at least a handful of regulars would be waiting to come in.

"I'm opening up!" I called, getting a few grunts and 'sounds good' in return. Not two minutes later people began trickling in until the place was swimming with patrons as it always was on a Friday night. A few pack mates waved as they made their way to a corner booth. I lifted a hand in greeting and said I'd be right over before dropping off a refill to Arya.

"Do you really think that Arya needs that second vodka cranberry?" The telltale chill of Theo's presence brushed my side and he fell into step beside me. My wolf preened at his presence. She always perked up when he was near, but, to be fair, so did I. He didn't break his stride as he walked straight through a table of elders to keep pace.

Freaking ghosts.

"Do you really think I want half the pack thinking I've lost my mind talking to empty air?" I asked through a smile, "We've talked about this Theo, at least wait until I'm back behind the bar."

"We both know I have far too many things to say to wait until then, and you're avoiding the question because you know you're enabling her poor choices," he said with a grin, two dimples appearing upon his iridescent skin, "You also know you're going to feel guilty about it later which means I'll be stuck listening to you worry about her tomorrow morning instead of praising the brunch I had planned for us."

"You can't even eat." I ignored his open-mouthed outrage and grabbed the notepad from my apron as I greeted my new table.

"That's incredibly rude to point out," he continued, "you know that's why I have to live vicariously through you."

I didn't respond back to him, but the smile on my face did grow a bit wider as I wrote down my table's order. I knew it had taken more than a little effort for Theo to perfect channeling his energy to move a single object, let alone cook a meal in my kitchen without breaking or burning anything. May the many bowls and plates that were sacrificed to the cause rest in peace.

"And to think I was going to make you cinnamon rolls," he grumbled.

I was definitely still getting those cinnamon rolls, hopefully with a side of potatoes too. It seemed like feeding me had become his favorite hobby over the years. If I was going to have a ghost haunting my house, at least it was a handsome ghost who came with perks. I couldn't remember the last time I had touched the stove or dusted the house. I firmly believed dusting was a task created by the devil.

"I'll get that order right in for you and be back with your drinks," I told the guys at the table before pivoting to drop their ticket in the kitchen and head back to the bar. I gave Arya's glass a quick peek as I passed and was pleasantly surprised to see it was still three quarters full.

"What were you saying about enabling?" I asked Theo

under my breath as I filled my table's first pitcher of beer. "Looks to me like she's handling herself just fine."

"Fine for now, at least," he conceded before leaning against the bar beside me, arms flexing where they crossed over his chest. I'd be lying if I said I'd never noticed them before, that I didn't intentionally steal a glance every time he held them that way.

I'd noticed a lot of things about it Theo over the past seven years—the way his lips held a slight perpetual pout, how his hair fell into his eyes when he turned his head too quickly, the glint that appeared in them when he teased me— but the most important thing I'd noticed, really the only thing that mattered, was he never changed.

Theo was frozen in time, and me? I was aging.

So what point would there be in noticing anything else?

"Give her a break, her date was god awful even by her standards. She deserves to let loose with an extra drink if she feels like it, and she won't be driving."

"What kind of awful?" He pushed away from the bar and turned to face me fully. "Did he hurt her? What's this guy's name?"

"What," I snorted, "are you going to pay him a visit if he did?"

The witty retort about knowing how to haunt a house I expected from him never came. When I looked up, all humor drained from his face as his brows drew in and his mouth settled in a firm line.

"I'm being serious," he said then asked again, "Did something happen to her on the date?"

"Hey, no. Nothing like that. She's completely fine," I assured him, hoping those creases between his brows would stop marring his skin. Not that he'd get wrinkled from it. Ghost benefits for the win.

I set the now full pitcher down on the bar and turned my back on the dining room and said, "The guy just was a sleaze ball but he didn't lay a hand on her. He probably wouldn't still have it if he did."

"Yeah, Beckett probably would've torn it off by now," he agreed on a sigh.

"I was more so thinking that Arya would have bitten it off, but Beck would probably be third in line to handle it if needed."

"I'm glad you know I'd be second." One side of his mouth lifted.

"Actually, I put you fourth."

If cackling alone behind the bar wouldn't draw unwanted attention the look of outrage on his face would've had me doubled over.

"Never mind that you ranked me behind our little Alpha." Beckett was anything but little. "Who exactly did you put ahead of us?"

I spun around to grab a tray from underneath the bar to load the pitcher and glasses. As I walked past him I quirked a brow and whispered, "Me."

The answering smile that stretched over Theo's face bordered on being reverent, and I found myself happy I never had to doubt it was meant for anyone but me. A lock of hair was tucked behind my ear without either of us lifting a finger.

I used to hate it when he did that. Now it sent a jolt to my chest.

"Bloodthirsty looks surprisingly good on you." His eyes raked over my body from my head down to my toes.

I did not blush.

"See what happens if you don't make those cinnamon rolls tomorrow, then tell me if you still like how it looks on me."

"If you still think that threat is a deterrent, you don't know me as well as I hoped," he countered, stepping closer as a smirk took over his face, "If you did, you'd know there's little I like more than seeing your fiery side come out to play."

"And after seven years together, you're still not tired of playing the same games with me?" I asked, in an equally wry tone, "I'm almost disappointed Theo. Does that mean I've seen all of your tricks?"

"Darling, I can promise you," he practically purred as he lowered his voice, "You haven't seen half the things I'd like to show you."

"So much talk yet so little action." I clucked my tongue and added, "I'll believe it when I see it."

"Is that a dare?" Theo asked, his eyes searching mine. It was a dangerous game we were playing, these moments of harmless flirtation that always seemed to border on something more.

"It's whatever you want it to be," I said lightly before gliding past him.

His gaze was warm on my back as I walked away. I knew if I peeked over my shoulder he'd be standing there, staring at me in a way I was having a harder and harder time not noticing. I'd only wanted one other person to look at me that way in the past.

The aftermath of that disaster was reminder enough not to wish for things I had no business wanting. I'd already had to leave my pack and start over once. I wasn't interested in doing it again, and something told me no matter where I went, there was a blond-haired ghost ready to follow me regardless of our standing.

That was the thing about being the only person who could see a ghost—they tended to get attached, or so it seemed. Theo was the only one I'd ever met. He'd scared me to high water and back when I found him sitting in the bay window of my living room on move-in day. His shock had rivaled my own. It took a few weeks of failed exorcisms and arguments, but we eventually found our way to a peaceful coexistence that turned into one of my most cherished friendships.

My shift was going like any other Friday night. People were cheerfully milling in and out, some of them cheerfully sharing their plans for the holiday. Arya sat chatting with me at the bar as she nursed her drink and grumbled about Valentine's Day being a stupid thing to celebrate anyway. A drunken fool or two occasionally got handsy with me, only for Theo to send a shock to their hands, and I made excuses about static electricity. All was normal at Howl, and then a rowdy group of males burst through the front door.

"I guess the bachelor party is here." Paisley propped her tray full of dishes she'd cleared from a six-top as we watched the group claim a few tables in her section.

"Go ahead and give that to me while you get them started on drinks," I offered, reaching for the tray, "I'll drop it off then make sure we don't need to bring up anything else to restock the bar."

It would be just our luck for one of the kegs to run dry in the middle of a rush.

"You're the best, Willow," she said with a sunny smile before practically dancing over to the newcomers. At this distance in the dim lighting of the bar I couldn't see any of their faces, and I absentmindedly wondered which pack they were visiting from.

After I dropped the plates and glasses off with the dishwasher, I had every intention of checking the bar like I'd promised. Those plans were brought to an abrupt halt when I pushed through the kitchen door only to find myself running face first into a flannel-covered brick wall of a man.

"Jeez Beck," I complained, rubbing my face, "Can you let like a millimeter of fat accumulate on your body? Your stupid pectorals almost broke my nose."

While I'd never accuse Beckett of being exuberant, I at least expected a twitch of his lip or an eye roll. Instead, all I got from the Alpha was a stern stare and a half-whispered, half-growled, "I've been trying to reach you for the last two hours. Why the hell haven't you been responding to my messages?"

"I left my phone in the car," I explained. Perplexed as to

why he hadn't just called the bar if he needed to speak to me I decided to ask as much. He ran his fingers through his hair in a gesture I knew meant he was frustrated, though because of what I didn't know.

"Because if I called you, then the reason I was calling you would know that I was doing it." Because that non-explanation cleared up all the confusion on my end.

"Has Beckett lost his mind?" Came Theo's whisper question over my shoulder, his mouth close enough to my ear I could feel his coldness brush against it even if I could never feel his breath. "Did Arya finally make him snap?"

Both valid questions, but I settled for a simple, "What are you talking about?"

"It's the bachelor party," he began to explain, "You know I let the Betas handle territory movements instead of reviewing them myself. I swear I didn't realize until this evening which packs had members visiting, or I would've said something. One of them is—"

Don't say Thornbridge, I silently pleaded, *say anything other than Thornbridge.*

"The Thornbridge Pack."

Of course it was.

Dread pooled in my stomach, but I didn't have a chance to ask which of the pack's members were here. Before I could even open my mouth to respond I was struck frozen by two golden brown eyes staring at me over Beckett's shoulder.

They were followed by an achingly familiar voice that said, "Hey, Low. It's been a long time."

CHAPTER 2

Willow

"Did he just call you, Low?" Theo asked. I didn't turn to look at him, but I could practically hear his upper lip curling. "You nearly bit my head off when I called you that, and we've been living together for years. Who is this guy to you?"

And for the first time in nearly a decade, the reason why the nickname set my teeth on edge was standing right in front of me. My wolf growled at the wolf she'd once considered her mate. Eight years hadn't been nearly long enough to dampen her ire.

"Rory," I acknowledged the towering man, but didn't pretend to share his sentiment that it was good to see him again. It wasn't. "Or I suppose I should address you as Alpha now, right?"

Even in this low light I could tell the tips of his ears grew just the slightest bit red.

"We don't need formalities between us," he said. In my

opinion we didn't need anything between us except distance. Preferably a lot of it. "I'm not here in any official capacity."

"Right. You're here to celebrate." I glanced over at the jovial tables his friends—at least some of which were my former pack mates—were laughing with one another as they gave Paisley their orders. "Well, it looks like Paisley will be taking great care of you all, so if you need anything, just wave her down."

"That's not why—" There wasn't a single thing he could say that would make me want to stay and listen. He was here. He'd made his presence known. Now I hoped we could go on pretending the other ceased to exist.

"If that's everything, I've got a few things in the back that need checking over. This place doesn't run itself, and we have a big crowd tonight."

It was incredibly rude for me to blow off, let alone speak over, any ranked shifter from another pack—especially if that shifter was an Alpha. When I looked to Beckett for a sign I was good to go, I could've sworn there was a sparkle of humor in his eye on an otherwise impassive face rather than the reproach or disappointment I expected. A small nod of his head was all I needed to start moving.

I saw no need for goodbyes. No good had come of them at our last parting. There was no reason to expect they would now.

"Low, wait." Rory's hand reached out to stop me, his fingers overlapping where they encircled my wrist. His grip wasn't painful, if anything it was gentle, but it was firm.

Two growls echoed around me, only one of which Rory

could actually hear. By the way he abruptly released me and shook out his hand, I suspected Theo had communicated his displeasure through other means. Sometimes having a ghost on hand was more effective than having a taser.

"What the hell?" Rory muttered, glancing between his hand and me.

Beck's face turned a shade closer to pasty as he mumbled, "Did you bring that damn ghost in my bar again?"

"Don't let him fool you," Theo draped his arm over my shoulder, and while I couldn't feel its weight, I leaned into the familiar chill, "He loves me, he's just still learning to accept it."

At my sheepish shrug, Beck added, "Damnit, Willow I told you to make sure that thing stays at home from now on. Just because you're content to be haunted doesn't mean the rest of us want to be too."

Theo leaned his head to rest atop of mine and said, "Poor guy's still in denial. He wishes he could be haunted by me."

"I'm sorry," Rory interjected, "Did you just say a ghost is haunting her?"

"He did," I said with a wave of my hand, "but that's really not relevant."

Rory looked from me to Beckett and back to me before shaking his head doubtfully, "Is this some kind of joke? Because if it is, I really don't get the punchline."

"Not a joke," Beckett confirmed, "Willow's had a ghost hanging around since she moved here, as crazy as that may sound."

"Why am I finding that a little hard to believe?" Rory ran

a hand through his chestnut brown hair with a smile, "And if you say it's because I ghosted you, I'll remind you that you're the one who left the pack. So if anyone ghosted someone it's you."

As if I'd had a choice.

"We're being perfectly literal," I assured him, growing irritated the longer I had to stand in his presence. My skin was beginning to itch from his proximity. My irritation was only amplified by my wolf's, and she was begging for me to change right here and now. I kept her contained. Rory's blood would be a pain to clean off the wooden floor. "Do you want him to shock you again to prove it? I doubt either of us would be opposed."

"Quite the opposite, in fact," Theo agreed.

"I don't think that'll be—" Beckett's protest was cut short when Rory jolted back a step as he rubbed his jawline, "necessary."

He sighed as though admitting defeat, and Theo's face lit up with a wicked grin.

"This thing lives with you?" Rory asked, still rubbing his jaw, "Has it harmed you?"

Not knowingly, and far less than you ever did, I wanted to say but didn't. I held back the first half for my own self-preservation. The second, because what use was there in reliving the past when there could be no changing the present?

"Of course he hasn't," I said instead. It was growing more and more obvious I wasn't escaping this conversation anytime soon. I took a deep breath, hoping to center both myself and my wolf. If I let her, she'd shift and claw at Rory's pretty face.

Two lines appeared between Rory's brows as he asked, "He? The ghost following you around, *living* with you, is a man?"

"Does he still believe in bleeding people when they're sick, because his views seem to be a bit outdated," my ghost observed, "Tell him I like to watch you sleep like that creepy vampire guy from that book you love, maybe that vein in his forehead will pop. If it does, we should definitely make Beck clean up the blood. It'd be his punishment for denying his love for me. Consequences are hard to deal with, but they're the only way for him to learn."

Even with the gnawing sensation in my stomach growing more pronounced the longer Rory's eyes bore into me, I couldn't help but grin. The man was truly one of a kind. At my small smile, his features transformed into the picture of smug satisfaction.

"I hate when it talks to you." Beckett shuddered and glanced away as if looking in the other direction would keep him from the ghost's presence. Little did he know Theo often followed him around all night in a one-sided conversation and had, for all intents and purposes appointed Beckett as his best friend. Other than me of course, but our relationship was a little bit, well, layered.

Because what do you call the only person in the world who could see and speak to you? Some days, usually during my more mopey time of the month, I wondered if we both felt the connection between us or if it was simply that his only other choice was returning to his life—or rather his existence—of solitude. If we'd met under normal circumstances, ones where he wasn't a ghost, in something mundane like a cafe on a rainy day, would he have even looked my way? I'd never know, and sometimes the not-knowing haunted me more than the ghost himself.

"I am not an *it*," the ghost in question stated, "I assure you I am very much a he. He's lucky I can't prove it to him."

I raised a brow in his direction, and he grinned. He was more than welcome to prove it to me any time.

"He doesn't appreciate your tone," I told Beckett, but my Alpha wasn't listening. His gaze was locked on a certain woman with cherry red hair at the bar. A male I'd never met before was twirling a lock of her hair as she sipped the most recent cocktail I'd made for her.

"If you'll excuse me for a moment, I have a pack member in need of attention," he deadpanned.

"She seems to be getting plenty as it is," I quipped, "but I doubt she'd mind a little more." Except if it was from Beckett, then she likely would. As skillful as Arya was at getting under his skin, he was every bit as talented at setting hers on fire. She may never admit it, but I saw the spark in her eyes whenever their wills collided.

Beck paused before taking a second step, turned to me, and asked, "You're good with him here?"

His eyes shifted briefly to the other Alpha who, if I wasn't mistaken, was now staring at me like I was a mirage he expected to dissipate if he glanced away. To be fair, I planned to disappear from his view as soon as the opportunity presented itself, so the expression was justified.

"We'll be just fine," I said, "Rory has said hello and is about to join his friends at that table. I'll be restocking the bar any second now. Go interfere in my best friend's love life."

"I'm not interfering, I'm just making sure she doesn't leave here with some creep," he argued, a scowl taking over his angular face.

"Whatever you say, Alpha," I gave a mock salute and took pleasure in his answering eye roll. I'd have been reprimanded if not fully disciplined for such a remark in other packs, but Beckett wasn't interested in leading mindless soldiers too afraid to anger him to have a personality.

"I don't need to remind you that this is my pack's territory," he said in a low voice as he passed by Rory, "and Willow is one of my wolves."

"Then why are you?" The other Alpha challenged cocking his head to one side, "I can promise you I'm not a threat to her."

"At least not one I can't handle," I added even though I wasn't certain that was true.

I used to look at Rory and think I was staring at my future, now all I saw was a past full of pain. I thought I'd locked those emotions away for good the day I got in my car and left, but they were starting to push the lid from the box. Sneaky little bastards.

"Or that I can't eliminate if the need arises," Theo offered, "Maybe if he died I could slip into his body.

Wouldn't that be interesting, me leading a pack you clearly have an issue with?"

"Absolutely not," I said pointing a finger in his face, momentarily not caring that any onlookers would likely think me insane, or drunk.

"Don't worry, I'd bring you with me to exact your revenge," he said with a smile.

"That is not the part I objected to and you damn well know it."

"Do I even want to know what he's saying?" Rory asked, pulling my attention from the ghost still sporting a shit-eating grin.

"Probably about as much as I want to hear what you're saying." He flinched, as if my words actually meant something to him. If that were the case, we wouldn't have even been here discussing a ghost in the first place. I would have never left. "I really do need to get back to work. You said your obligatory hello or whatever this is, so let's just head to our respective spots in the bar and go back to pretending the other doesn't exist, okay? Enjoy the party."

"I didn't just come here for the party," he said.

"Of course he didn't," Theo grumbled.

"I actually suggested this territory because I heard you'd moved here." Rory reached back to rub his hand along the back of his neck as he added, "I wasn't even sure if it was true, but I had to at least try."

What in the actual fuck?

"And why would you be looking for me? We both know you're not here to ask me to be your Valentine," I gestured to the decorations we'd hung on the back wall the night before. The whole town was practically dripping in hearts and lace. I'd be surprised Beck allowed it in the bar if I hadn't heard Arya lamenting the lack of decorations the year prior. "So what is it?"

Each word that left his mouth was perfectly measured. His eyes tracked me like a doe would track out wolves. "Something is tormenting the pack. Strange things are happening. Strange things like the things that happened before you left."

Ice danced along my spine.

This time Theo's presence had nothing to do with it.

"Did you ask Miles about it?" I asked with as little emotion as I could manage. God I hoped that asshole hadn't come with him tonight.

"I know you think Miles had something to do with what happened before Faye disappeared." It was unbelievable, that even now he was still questioning it—questioning me. "But he didn't. He couldn't have, and I think deep down you know it. He loved her."

"Disappearance?" I asked, ignoring his claims about Miles. This was the first time I'd heard anyone from that pack —my family included—imply I could've been telling the truth about what happened that day. "Didn't you tell me she *must* have been killed? That I *must* have made up what I saw?"

He gave no answer.

"Didn't the entire pack say that I *must* be lying to cover up my own actions?" Still, silence was his only answer.

"You refused to listen to me then, so why are you here now?"

Rory at least had the good grace to show the slightest hint of shame on his too-beautiful face as he considered his answer. He wouldn't apologize—Alphas never did—but a tiny piece of me hoped he felt regret over what happened. He may not have directly pushed me out of the pack, but he'd done nothing to stop the others. He'd done nothing to defend me at all. He'd simply turned his back.

"You have to know how it looked at the time," he said imploringly, "Everyone knew you'd had a falling out. You were practically at each other's throats the second you were within half a mile of each other."

"So an ended friendship is all it takes to convince you I would kill someone and hide the body without remorse?"

"The two of you went into the woods, and you were the only one to return. That clearing was practically leveled," he argued, "She was enraged when you were chosen as an Enforcer in her place, and you know it. Is it really so shocking we'd think she challenged you and lost?"

"I told you what happened in that clearing." It was exactly what I'd told everyone else. "And if I'd killed someone in a challenge it would've been well within my right. There'd be no reason for me to hide it."

"You would if you—damnit!" He broke off as he grasped his cheek yet again, "Call off your damn ghost."

"I don't like him," Theo said, his face uncharacteristically stoic. "Do you want me to give him a heart attack? I could still try snatching his body."

"No body snatching," I told him, only slightly enjoying the horror that crossed Rory's face. My wolf was practically salivating at the idea, but I didn't want Theo here, witnessing my past get rehashed. "I'll keep you posted on that other offer. I've got this. Can you just give us a few minutes, please?"

Theo looked Rory up and down before giving a reluctant nod of his head, "Call me if you need me. I won't be far."

He never was.

Turning back to the visiting Alpha, I said, "I have no desire to relive the history between us. I don't even know why you came here when it's obvious nothing has changed. You still can't admit there's no world in which I would have killed another pack mate, so what is there left to discuss?"

"I saw a red cloak with gold embroidery."

Black spots began to invade the edges of my vision. I told the pack someone in that cloak had taken Faye when we were in the clearing. None of them had believed me. For that garment to make an appearance years later couldn't— shouldn't—be possible.

"I saw it in the tree line during Emma's birthday celebration." Faye's sister would've just turned twenty. She was coming of age, just like we'd been. "By the time I made it through the crowd, whoever it was had already disappeared."

"You said strange things were happening in the pack again," I said slowly, "Tell me, how often has Miles been hanging around Emma these days."

Rory's eyes narrowed as he shook his head, "I already told

you this isn't Miles. He looks out for Emma like a little sister."

Meaning he'd chosen to bide his time and wait for the younger sister to grow up now that the elder was out of reach.

"I have nothing to offer you," I told him truthfully, "You should go back to your party then leave this territory. Go back to forgetting I exist." So I can go back to pretending to forget that he did.

"Please, Willow." His lips wrapped around my name like a whispered prayer. "I need your help."

"Yeah?" I asked, stepping through the door to the storage room, "And where were you when I needed yours?"

I swung the door shut, closing it on both his regret-filled face and the buried memories it threatened to unearth.

CHAPTER 3

Willow

"It took him so long to walk through the door, that for a second I wondered if he was a sloth shifter instead of a wolf, but he's finally gone," Theo informed me as he hopped onto the counter in the back room. I'd spent half the night there tackling tasks that probably should've waited until a weekday.

"Good." Let that be the end of us.

The group of males with Rory had stayed through the last call. I'd avoided speaking to him again by sending Paisley over to their table more often than was necessary and stopping by tables on the opposite side of the restaurant as much as possible. I'd felt his eyes tracking each step that I took. Even if I hadn't, Theo's running commentary would've kept me well informed.

"So are you planning to explain who he is to you at some point?" Theo tilted his head to the side expectantly.

"Nope," I said.

I grabbed the spray bottle and a rag and headed to the door, but he slid off the counter and into my path before I made it more than a few feet. I could technically walk through him to leave, but that was more than a little bit disrespectful when it came to ghosts—at least in my limited experience with this one.

"It was pretty obvious he's more than just a former pack mate, darling," he said, "So what is he? Childhood best friend? First love?"

"He's no one we need to discuss, and he's gone now," I protested, but it didn't deter him from continuing his line of questioning.

"Former stalker? You can tell me if he was the pack pervert. I have a special way of handling those."

His blabbering brought a reluctant grin to my face despite my attempts not to give in to his playful probing. I knew what he was doing. One of Theo's superpowers was making me lower my guard with quips and jokes until I felt so comfortable I'd happily share the darkest secrets of my soul if he asked it of me. When humor didn't work he'd typically resort to stronger means of persuasion—ice cream and cozy cups of tea.

But just because I knew what he was doing didn't mean it wasn't working. I couldn't be positive what color Theo's eyes had been when he was still walking the earth, but I imagined they were warm. When he turned them on me and they softened ever so slightly like they were right then, he could ask me to snuggle a cat and I'd gladly suffer the runny nose and hives.

"He's not a pervert and he definitely didn't stalk me." If anything I'd been the one borderline stalking him. "He just reminds me of things I'd rather forget."

"You know what's great for forgetting things?" he asked. I was almost afraid to ask.

"Tea and chocolate?" I suggested.

"Telling someone else."

"That would be the exact opposite of forgetting something. That would be spreading it and letting it live on through others," I argued.

Theo waved his hand dismissively as he went on to explain, "It's not. Whatever this is, it's obviously bothering you. You looked like you were ready to either claw at his face or flee the country when you saw him. If I had to pick, I'd never pass up the chance to watch you cut into someone, but even that's not worth seeing you look cornered."

For the record, I hadn't *technically* clawed anyone in years, but if I had, they'd definitely deserved it.

"Your love of violence is mildly concerning sometimes." He'd looked far too pleased at the idea. "Can't you just act like a normal person and pester me with questions if you're going to be nosy?"

"Says the shifter to the ghost. I think we surpassed normal quite a while ago, don't you?" A fair point. He took one step closer to me and said more seriously, "Whatever this is, it's eating away at you, and I don't like it. So why don't you share it with me and it can try to eat away at me instead? I'm basically made of air these days, so it'll be distracted chomping for the foreseeable future."

"So you're the low calorie option?" I asked.

"Exactly," he agreed easily, "Now stop deflecting."

"Can you just drop it?" I asked in exasperation as I looked to the ceiling—I don't know why I always looked up when praying for patience, all I saw there was an old ceiling. "Go feed the dog if you need something to amuse yourself with."

"Skye is your dog, why am I the one always feeding her?" He uncrossed his arms to plant them on his trim hips.

"Because you're the one who was so determined I adopt her," I pointed out.

And thank god he had. I couldn't imagine life without my girl now that I had her. Once I got past all the shedding, I totally got the hype around golden retrievers. They really were a woman's—and ghost's—best friend.

"I did that for you," he argued, "I didn't want your wolf to get lonely."

"For the last time, Theo," I said, "I can't speak dog in my wolf form! Plus my wolf isn't lonely, she has an entire pack plus you hanging around twenty-four seven."

"Yes, but who does she confide her secrets in? Everyone needs a person to confide in, which, as we were *just* discussing, is why you have me, but wolfie Willow deserves to have a friend too."

Damn him and his ability to circle the conversation back to where I didn't want it to be. If I didn't know better I'd say *he* was the canine between us because he was certainly going after that bone.

"I really don't have time to get into this right now, Theo. I need to start wiping down the bar and tables."

I lifted the spray bottle and rag to emphasize that there were, in fact, matters to be handled. Matters that had nothing to do with a six foot Alpha with chestnut hair and honey-brown eyes that used to star in my every daydream.

"That's easily remedied." Theo snapped his fingers and the cleaning supplies were pulled from my hands and flying through the now-open door, which shut with a resounding click a moment later.

"Are you kidding me with this?" Beckett called, "What did I say about bringing that ghost in my bar? Leave him at home!"

The melodic sound of Arya's voice snapping back at him was too muffled by the wooden barrier for me to make out the words, but by the tone I imagined it was something along the lines of not to turn down free labor—that or to get over himself.

"He's obviously very grateful for my help," Theo said in a shockingly sincere tone, "and now that the cleaning has been taken care of, please Willow, just tell me what's going on."

Telling him—telling anyone was risky. I'd never explained everything that happened that night, at least not fully. If I did, everything I'd worked so hard to protect—to keep hidden—would be at risk.

They say that the only way two people can keep a secret is if one of them is dead. Maybe they were right, but what if the dead one had a propensity for chatter?

I may be the only person who could see and hear Theo,

at least that we knew of, but what if someone else with the ability eventually came along? Maybe if I understood why I could communicate with him it would be safer. Then I could at least try to predict who else may have the gift, but I didn't.

I knew he wouldn't betray me intentionally but it would only take one person overhearing our conversation for all of it to come crumbling down.

But I had to at least tell him *something*. His worry for me was evident in the faint creases at the corner of his eyes, in the tapping of his fingertips against his thumb. I doubt he even noticed he was doing the nervous action.

"I wasn't always part of the Sun Meadow Pack," I began to explain. Theo raised a single brow as if to say no shit, but refrained from interrupting me as I went on to say, "I grew up in the Thornbridge Pack with Rory, which you've obviously already pieced together."

He nodded but still said nothing, instead choosing to wait patiently for me to continue my story. It'd been an unspoken rule between us before now—that I wouldn't ask him how he died and he wouldn't ask me where I'd escaped from when I joined the pack—but I couldn't blame him for being curious when my past showed up right in front of us.

"Rory's parents were the Alpha and Luna of the pack, and my parents were their Betas so naturally, we spent more than a little time together growing up. We were also always with the Head Enforcer's daughter, Faye, my best friend. The three of us were as close as a group of kids could be until we got into our late teens. Rory had always been popular, but he'd really begun to come into his own after puberty. It was never a question that he'd become the next Alpha after his father, but the stronger he grew, the more the others flocked to him. Everyone wanted to be in his inner circle, including another Enforcer's son, Miles."

I took a deep breath before diving into what happened next.

"I never liked Miles," I said seriously, "Not even when we were children. He seemed charming to others, but to me he felt like a snake waiting to shed his skin, and once he had his fangs in Rory, it was like he considered himself untouchable. He had little interest in me, but Faye wasn't as lucky."

Phantom fingers wrapped around my own, one running along the back of my hand in soothing strokes that would have me melting under any other circumstance.

"She thought he was just another suitor. Rory loved him, her parents loved him, the entire pack loved him except me, so how could she not love him as well?"

She didn't see it at first. I should have made her, but by the time she did it was too late.

"But then strange things started happening—both to her and others in the pack. I could never prove it to the others, but I'm positive it was because of Miles' obsession with her. There were cryptic notes left in her locker at school. Weapons and potions went missing from the pack store-house. Flowers without a note were delivered to her house each week; that would have been sweet and romantic, except they were poisonous. Then finally, blood-soaked gifts started showing up on her doorstep—probably trophies from his wolf for hers. After that it was like he started showing up everywhere we went."

I cringed as I remembered each time we saw flashes of his face on street corners or between aisles at the grocery store. Sometimes he'd disappear quickly, others he would linger and stare unabashedly.

"What happened next, darling?" Theo asked in a whisper, bringing me out of the memories.

"Faye and I had a fight." I ignored the way my voice cracked at the end. "When I look back on it, all I can think is how stupid it was. In the Thornbridge Pack we're selected to train for our future roles when we come of age at twenty. Anyone hoping for a role stayed in the pack after high school wanting to prove ourselves and took online classes while the rest went off to college. She and I both hoped to become Enforcers, but she wasn't selected. I was."

"She was angry," he guessed.

"Furious." Or something beyond furious. "It was like the straw that broke her back, you know? I think she already felt so powerless with the issues with Miles that this was like losing her last scrap of power over her own life. Her father's status as Head Enforcer only added insult to injury when the Alpha and Luna chose not to appoint her."

"And Miles?" Theo asked through gritted teeth, "What rank was he given?"

"Beta."

"Of course," he mumbled, shaking his head.

"I don't know all the details of what happened next," I admitted, "Faye had completely shut me out by then, but I could see enough from afar to know it only got worse. Without a rank her parents began pushing her toward Miles even harder. At least at his side she'd be a Beta Mate rather than a lowly, normal pack member."

"Why wasn't she chosen?" Nausea grew in my gut at the question I'd asked myself a hundred times over.

"I can't be sure," I said slowly, "But my guess is it's because Rory asked his parents not to select her."

"Because of Miles," he surmised without me having to spell it out for him.

"Yes. Rory is the only person with his parents' ear that would even consider rejecting Faye, and given he'd eventually lead the pack with Miles at his side, it's not surprising he'd be given a say in our appointments. The incoming Luna wouldn't have cared either way. She was making plans for her own ranks."

"Appointments can change though, can't they?" Theo asked, and I almost laughed at the innocence of the question.

"They can, usually due to someone slandering or scheming against someone else to discredit them. It's a risky move though, because if you fail you're the one who is discredited. Pack politics are a blood bath." Sometimes literally. "If someone is ready to risk it all though, they'll issue a challenge to the person they want to replace directly."

"And Faye issued you a challenge?"

"No," I said emphatically, "The pack only thinks she did."

"Okay, I need you to just keep talking because I can only

ask why so many times and it not get awkwardly repetitive. I'm a ghost, not a parrot."

That had my lips twitching. "I don't know, I think you'd look cute with some feathers."

"I look cute in anything." I didn't doubt it. "Now tell me about this challenge that never happened."

"I saw Faye going into the woods one day alone and decided to follow her," I recited the same words I'd told my former pack mates a hundred times over. "I was worried about her. It seemed like the dark circles under her eyes were a permanent fixture, and I'd never seen her so skinny. When she checked over her shoulder as she went, I saw her face and followed her. She looked scared."

She had every right to be.

I was scared too.

"I followed her deeper and deeper into the woods. I wasn't sure if she was running away or just needed some time and space, but whatever it was, I had an awful feeling that grew the farther we went. Then I heard her scream."

I shuddered imagining the shrill sound cutting through the air.

"She was faster than me," I admitted, "I was stronger, but she was faster and I'd fallen too far behind to see everything that happened. When I reached the clearing, it was a picture of destruction. There were broken trees and divots in the dirt."

I looked up into Theo's eyes and said, "And there was blood. Through the tree line I saw a figure carrying her limp body over their shoulder. I yelled and ran after them but something struck me from behind. The next thing I knew I was waking up on the ground at nightfall. Alone."

I didn't realize I would still be alone even after I made it back to the pack.

"I'm so sorry, Willow," Theo said, an earnest warmth coloring his voice, "I'm sorry you lost your best friend, especially when you were so young. What I'm struggling to get though is what this has to do with the tension between you and the Alpha-hole. Did you blame him? Do you think Miles abducted her when she wouldn't be with him willingly?"

"I didn't blame Rory, it's more that he and everyone else blamed me." I paused before I spoke, choosing my next words carefully. "I don't know if Miles wanted to have her abducted or punish her for rejecting him, but his behavior is undoubtedly what drove her into those woods. I'm just the only one to think so."

"No one believed you." He shook his head, hair falling across his forehead as he realized, "Your pack didn't believe you. They thought you killed her in a challenge."

"Yes."

All of them, even my own family, but I didn't share that particularly painful detail. I was being laid bare enough as it was.

Theo wrapped his arms around me, and I leaned into the coolness of his not-quite touch.

"Then fuck them," he said decidedly, "Fuck them for driving you away, and fuck that Alpha for coming here after they did it. You don't owe anything to any of them."

Except Faye.

Her, I still felt like I owed everything.

I'D BEEN LYING IN BED, MY SIXTY POUNDS OF golden fluff curled up and taking more than her fair share of the space beside me for hours and—despite the fact I had counted every sheep, lizard, gorilla, and capybara—I still couldn't fall asleep. Not even the sleepy time tea Theo had made me before bed was strong enough to combat the debate that was currently taking place in my head.

Whatever was happening in the Thornbridge Pack, it wasn't my problem. I knew that, I did, but knowing it wasn't my problem didn't make it easier to turn off the waves of guilt and anxiety rolling over me. All I could see when I tried to close my eyes was Faye and her sister looking at me with matching smiles, matching midnight blue curls, as a shadow loomed over them.

I should've asked Rory for more details instead of rushing to escape him because of my own discomfort. What oddities was he seeing around the pack? Did they all center around Emma or were other members being targeted as well? What details were on the cloak? Surely someone wouldn't be so stupid that they'd wear the same garment around the pack eight years later.

Now that he wasn't standing in front of me, the walking embodiment of everything I had once wanted and lost, I could understand that something must have been seriously wrong if he chose to come all the way here after all this time.

It should've been obvious by the lines around his tired eyes and the stiff set of his lips. He'd lost the confident, care-free aura he'd had when I last saw him.

Well, maybe not the last time. The last time he'd berated me for choosing to leave rather than own up to my own mistakes. Funny how even now he still hadn't owned up to his. In fact, if I saw him again I'd like to—no. Rory being an absolute failure of a friend was not what mattered anymore.

I huffed loudly enough for Skye to briefly lift her head from my hip to glance at me before lying back down.

"Sorry, sweet girl," I said, running a hand along her back at my side, "I'll try to keep my frustration to myself."

It was decided. I'd put Rory, the Thornbridge Pack, and all of the questions and concerns that came with them out of my mind. I would stay in my new, happy life with my new pack mates, an Alpha I could actually trust, my golden fluff ball of joy, and my ghost without giving any of them another thought. I'd leave them all in the past where they belonged.

Except I wasn't sure I could.

But I *could* make sure I wasn't the only one cursed by a sleepless night. After all, he'd ruined my dreams.

It was only fair I returned the favor.

CHAPTER 4

Willow

A perk of being in a small pack was knowing all the local business owners—including the ones who ran the only inn in town. I was sure Martha, the woman who'd run this place for over twenty years, would have a rumor about my goings-on with the Thornbridge Pack Alpha flying around by daybreak. Unfortunately for me, calling her was the only way to get Rory's room number. I hadn't explained my request when I showed up at the front desk, but the rosy tint to her cheeks told me all I needed to know about what assumptions she'd drawn.

I didn't waste time correcting her. I had a wolf to wake.

Which is what I'd spent the last five minutes attempting to do by rapping my knuckles against his door. He always did sleep like the dead. I'd jumped onto his bed more than once to get him to wake up in time for school or to convince him to go into the city with me.

I pounded on the door once more before giving it a kick

for good measure. Nothing. Honestly, you'd think once he became Alpha he'd figure out how to be more alert to threats while he slept. I could've invaded half the territory by now.

"Rory Thompson, if I have to break down this door, you're going to regret it," I screamed. If I had to change into my wolf and claw down that door I was not going to be happy, though my wolf would be all too happy to cause a little destruction and let him foot the bill.

I was bracing myself for a second barrage of banging, when the door from the opposite side of the hall where a still-groggy voice said, "And just what is it you plan to do to me when you get through that door, Low?"

My back tensed straighter than a flag pole as I froze, my fist still raised a couple inches from the poor soul's door I'd been attacking. I hoped they weren't in, because the only alternative I could think of for them not to answer was they must be dead on the other side. I was lucky they hadn't called the Enforcers for help against the crazy lady shouting at them in the middle of the night. Beckett would be less than pleased and Arya would never let me live it down.

I pivoted around slowly, knowing my cheeks were already burning at being caught berating the wrong room, and a wave of something I didn't want to identify shot through me. A pajama-clad Rory was leaning against the doorway, ankles and arms crossed, looking like the picture of still-sleepy satisfaction. With pillow-tousled hair, clad in blue flannel pajama pants and a fitted white tee shirt that did nothing to hide the physique he'd obviously grown into during my absence, anyone's body would surely react the same as mine.

"Low?" he asked again, one sheet-imprinted cheek lifting as he did, "What were you going to do to me? I'm increasingly curious, especially when you're dressed like that."

Damnit.

My cheeks were definitely bordering on scarlet now. I became all too aware of the slight draft in the hall brushing against my skin. My vast expanses of exposed skin.

Because apparently when I hopped out of bed in the wee hours of the morning to give someone a piece of my mind, I didn't think changing out of the shorts and tank top I'd slept in was a top priority. God, no wonder Martha looked as smug as she did telling me which room to go to. I looked like his clandestine mistress visiting in the night.

I was tempted to cross my arms over my chest but resisted. It was too late to change now, so I guess I'd better own it, red cheeks, exposed thighs, and all. Rory was still leaning there, waiting for my response.

"You just be grateful you won't have to find out," I said with a confidence I didn't feel, "Now are you going to move your big body out of that door so I can come in, or what?"

His tongue briefly ran along his bottom lip as he paused to consider it, "I don't know, Low. Us alone in a hotel room in the middle of the night after such a commotion in the hall? What will the neighbors say?"

"Well I'm not going to murder you if that's what you're implying," I assured him dryly. I knew damn well what he was actually implying, but I wasn't touching that idea with a ten foot pole. "Contrary to popular belief, I've never killed anyone, though I'm starting to wonder if you'll be the first."

Though definitely not the kind of first I'd always thought he'd be.

"Right," he ran a hand over his head, making his already messy hair even messier, "Come on in then."

He took a step back to allow me to step through the door. I only hesitated the briefest of moments when my shoulder brushed his chest as I entered into the small but cozy room.

The bed was disheveled from where he'd presumably rolled out of it moments before, but everything else was the picture of spic and span. His suitcase was open, clothes folded neatly inside. Through the open door to the adjoining bathroom I could see his toiletries lined up along the counter's edge. His shoes were placed beside the door, and the unlit fireplace was free of ash. The only light was the soft glow of the lamp on the nightstand.

The automatic lock clicked as Rory shut the door behind me. He crossed the room to take a seat at the end of his bed. He rested his elbows on his widespread knees and gestured for me to take the armchair by the unlit fireplace before clasping his hands in the space in front of him.

"It's barely five in the morning, Low," he said once I'd taken my seat, "I've got nothing vying for my attention right now, so the floor is yours. What has you coming to bang down my door in your, let's call it, sleep-ready state?"

That was the problem. I was more than ready for sleep, sleep just wasn't ready for me.

"Tell me more about what's happening in the pack." His eyebrows lifted the tiniest amount, like he was surprised that was what I'd come here to ask. I didn't know why. Why else would I be showing up at his hotel room before dawn's first light? So we could braid each other's hair and catch up?

No thanks.

"What do you want to know?" Rory asked.

"Everything." Obviously. How else was I supposed to help him put the pieces together? I needed to know what we were really dealing with, and I couldn't get that from vague answers and broad statements.

"It started a few months ago," he began to explain, "At first, I wondered if some of the teenagers were just bored and getting into trouble for the heck of it. It was small things—things like bouquets showing up at Emma's home but the flowers were removed from the stems."

Not exactly like what had been sent to Faye, but definitely reminiscent of it.

"But it's not just issues surrounding her. Businesses of former Enforcers have had bricks thrown through windows, never when they were open, but still causing significant damage. The high school was defaced in the middle of the night. Even Miles' house has been hit by vandals a few times."

I can't say my heart went out to him. I hoped the house collapsed from the damages, preferably with him still inside.

"It's like someone has a score to settle with the pack," he said shaking his head, "but I can't figure out what it is. No one's been injured. No irrevocable damage has been done. If I hadn't glimpsed that cloak running through the tree line I would've been sure it was just a string of petty crimes."

Because a teenage girl receiving flowers with their heads essentially cut off was considered *petty*. I considered it *creepy*. *Disturbing. Red flag* behavior.

"Tell me more about the cloak," I prompted. I leaned back in the wing-backed chair as my fingers dug into the velvet of the arm rests. "You said there was gold embroidery on it?"

He nodded. "I couldn't see it perfectly from that distance but it looked like the bottom was covered in a web of golden vines. There may have been a few stars on it too but I couldn't tell."

Not stars. Flowers. Lilies, to be exact. I wouldn't be able to forget them even if I tried, but why had they returned?

"So?" he asked, "What do you think?"

"I think it sounds like you have a problem on your hands." And it was one that felt too familiar for comfort.

"Well," he drew the word out, "I think that's been established, but what hasn't been determined is if you're planning to help me with it or not."

If I were smart, I wouldn't. I would stay far away, both from Rory and the Thornbridge Pack. All that was waiting there for me there was disappointment and old dreams I wish I'd never had in the first place. Dreams like Rory waking up one day and realizing I was one who should be the Alpha Mate at his side—that I'd *always been* at his side, waiting for him to notice me there. Dreams like working alongside him and our peers to pick up where our parents left off and leading the pack into peace and prosperity.

Dreams that took a lifetime to build and a day to shatter.

"What do you want me to do?" I asked softly, "What exactly are you asking for here? A thought partner? Someone to validate you aren't crazy for being concerned? Do you need me to recap what happened that night for the two millionth time?"

Silence.

"What do you want from me, Rory?" I hoped it wasn't more than I could give. I hoped it wouldn't mean losing one of the few pieces of myself I hadn't already given in service of the woman who was, once upon time, my best friend.

"I want you to come back to Thornbridge with me."

The blood I felt draining from my face as pressure grew in my chest must have left my already pale skin even lighter because he quickly raised his hands in front of him as if to surrender.

"I'm not saying permanently." Ouch. It's not like I wanted to go back forever, but he could at least pretend the option was out there for me to reject.

"As if your pack wouldn't tar and feather me as soon as I crossed the border, even if I wanted to stay." Something like remorse flashed across his face, but it was gone too quickly to matter.

"I understand you wouldn't come back permanently even if I asked you to." Still, it would have been nice to actually *be* asked. "I'm just asking you to come back with me for a few days—a week, max—to see what we can piece together."

A week? An entire week of walking on eggshells looking for a threat in the woods around people who would happily exile me to them? Nothing about that sounded appealing to me. Except, what else could I do if what Rory described was true? I had to go there. I had to see it for myself.

"If I go." I was totally going. "Then I don't want to see anyone else, do you understand? I get that they'll be able to literally see me, but don't ask me to speak to anyone, have a meal with anyone, nothing."

"Willow, your parents are just—"

"I said, *nothing* and *no one*." And I meant it. "Or I'll just stay here and you can try to put a stop to this mystery yourself."

Giving any shifter an ultimatum was risky. It went against our very nature, like a challenge for dominance. But to give an ultimatum to an Alpha? That was damn near unheard of, but he wasn't my Alpha. It wasn't me reaching out to ask for help.

It was him who needed me, and I needed him to agree to this if I was going to risk going back. He didn't agree right away, not that his silence should have surprised me.

If he thought I would backtrack from the force of his stare alone he would be sorely disappointed and probably have annoyingly dry eyes. Blinking was important. It's why I lost all of our staring contests as a kid.

"Fine," he finally agreed. He pulled his elbows from his knees and shifted to lean back on the bed instead, "You won't have to speak to anyone but me. I'm sure we can find plenty to talk about."

"Yeah," I said, "Like why your lips are twitching while we discuss saving your pack from whatever threat it's facing. Is impending danger just that fun for you?"

I expected him to roll his eyes or smile and make a quip back, but that isn't what he did. No, what he did was far worse.

"With you? Yeah, I kind of think it could be." He looked me directly in the eye and said, "I really missed you, Low."

And really, when his eyes grew soft and he looked at me like nothing else existed in the soft glow of the lamp, what was I supposed to say in response?

It wasn't the time, it certainly wasn't the place, and it didn't change a single thing between us, but much to my–and my wolf's–dismay, I found myself admitting, "I missed you too."

If only 'I miss yous' were enough.

CHAPTER 5

Theo

Willow had gone to see the Alpha and returned ready to leave me behind.

Well, at least for a few days, or so she claimed. Shadows had appeared in her eyes the moment they landed on him in the bar, and I didn't like it. I didn't like the way he looked at her like he knew her better than he knew himself. I didn't like the way her body locked in discomfort when he called her that damn nickname. I definitely didn't like the slight color gracing the top of her cheeks when he drew near. I thought we'd agreed to put him and that awful pack in the past and continue on to our present and future.

I guess I'd been wrong.

Rather than finding her curled up with Skye when I'd popped in with a freshly baked cinnamon roll early this morning, I found an empty bed and a dog who looked at me as if to ask why I dared to disturb her slumber.

Skye didn't understand the beauty of breakfast in bed. To be fair, I hadn't fully appreciated it until it was no longer a luxury I could choose to enjoy. I had to live vicariously through Willow instead. Seeing her face light up when I delivered breakfast to her while she was still snuggled away may have been even better than experiencing it myself.

By the time she returned home, the cinnamon roll had gone cold where it waited for her on the kitchen table. I could have kept it warm in the oven with the rest of them, but sometimes people had to have consequences for their actions. How else would she learn that between the ghost baking in her kitchen and the wolf plaguing her doorstep, there was a clear answer as to which of us provided more value?

Except rather than walking in the door, seeing the abandoned treat and realizing the error of her ways, she'd gone straight to the attic. The half-dusty suitcase she'd retrieved from it was now open on her bed as she tossed occasional garments into it from where she stood just inside her closet door.

"And remind me, why exactly do we care about helping these people?" I flicked a finger in the air to remove the latest addition to the pile of clothes on her bed and folded the crumpled sweater before letting it settle neatly in her bag.

"We kind of don't," she called back, another shirt flying through the doorway, this one a henley, "But we also don't want an innocent girl's safety on our conscience."

I could live with that on my conscience if it meant she wouldn't leave.

"Besides," she added as she walked back into the room, "It's only for a few days."

I deliberately looked from her to the suitcase sporting enough clothing for a month's vacation and back.

"Are you sure about that?" I asked, because I certainly wasn't. Her lips quirked up in a sheepish grin that I'd find endearing under different circumstances.

"You know I'm an over-packer." It's true. She was. We once spent a weekend at the beach and she'd brought two sweatshirts in case the mornings were chilly. It would've been a reasonable choice if the trip wasn't in mid July. "I just want to be prepared."

As long as it wasn't to be prepared to stay. I hummed noncommittally and she chuckled.

"What?" she asked. "Are you going to be lost without me the two or three days I'm gone?"

"Yes." Without question.

Every day with her was like standing in the sunlight, and every day parted from her was like being stuck in the dead of night without a single star to wish upon. Willow didn't seem to realize that though, because despite the complete sincerity in my answer, her melodic laugh ran through the room as if I were joking.

"You're ridiculous." She waved a hand in the air dismissively and stepped back into the closet. A pair of jeans flew out a moment later.

I let them stay crumpled on the bed.

"Don't you just find it a little bit odd that this Alpha just waltzes into town and—"

"Willow!" The bang of the front door opening and Arya's shouting could have woken the dead if my eyes hadn't already been wide open.

"Oh good," I said as Willow popped her head out of the closet and looked toward what sounded like a stampede of elephant stomps ascending the stairs, "WD is here."

"Don't call her that," my little wolf said with a pointed finger just as we heard a thump and a groan from the stairwell.

"It's appropriate and you know it." I was fond of Arya. I liked the way she made Willow smile, and I liked the way she drove my best friend Beck a little bit insane, but the girl was a *walking disaster* through and through.

"Did you seriously visit the boy you spent your teen years mooning over in the middle of the night in nothing but your pajamas and *not* call your best friend about it before the whole damn pack knew?" Arya asked as she pushed through the door, rubbing her hip and adorably wrinkling her nose. She was a catastrophe but a cute catastrophe. Kind of like a baby chipmunk.

"Aren't you supposed to be at the animal shelter this afternoon?" Willow asked dryly, arms crossing under her chest.

Arya rolled her eyes and mimicked her pose, "They were over-staffed—some youth volunteer day thing—and don't change the subject! What the hell were you doing in Rory's room last night?"

I made myself comfortable on the bed, leaning against the headboard and waited for the answer. I'd been wondering that myself, but you could only ask a question so many times before you sounded like the jealous man you absolutely were.

"We had a few things we needed to discuss." No shit.

"Uh uh," WD protested, "I don't want any high level vague answers from you. I want details, and I want them right now."

She went so far as to stamp her boot-clad foot before stomping over to take a seat on the bed. Unfortunately for both of us, she chose the spot that just happened to coincide with my lap.

"And why is your room so cold?" Arya rubbed her hands up both her arms.

"Um, Ari?" Willow bit her beautifully full bottom lip trying not to chuckle. "That spot's occupied, love."

She looked confused for a moment until I took it upon myself to blow a small gust against her ear. Her shriek was both painful and satisfying as she rolled to the other side of the bed.

"Gosh, Theo can you not?" A shudder ran from the top of her head to the tips of her boots—boots she really shouldn't have on Willow's bed. It was rude. I did her a favor by removing them and stacking them neatly by the door.

"Okay mister manners," she grumbled, "If you were really that polite you would've moved when a lady went to sit down instead of holding still like a creeper."

"It's not my fault she chose my spot," I told my wolf, hands raised in the air, "She knows the other side of the bed is yours. She should've figured out this side would be mine."

"You don't have a side of the bed." Maybe not officially

but if one was hers, who else could own the other? Skye preferred sprawling across the middle, and I'd freeze that Alpha into an ice cube if he ever thought to claim it.

Except that would be selfish, wouldn't it? It's not like I could actually be the man sleeping next to her. First of all, I didn't sleep. Second of all, I wasn't even a solid man anymore, was I? Willow deserved someone who could hold her hand as they walked down the street. She deserved someone who could build a family with her if that's what she wanted, who could age with her.

While I believed Willow and I were happy for now in our roommates who make gah gah eyes state, she deserved to be happy forever. Forever was the one thing we couldn't promise each other.

That didn't mean the Alpha deserved to be in my place. He'd turned his back on her once already. I didn't trust him not to do it again. If I was going to give her up, I'd only give her up to someone who could come close to deserving her. From what I'd seen, he didn't make the list.

"Now tell what really happened in that hotel room," Arya demanded once again.

Willow turned to me and asked, "Are you planning to give me privacy for this conversation?"

"I can pretend to if that will make you feel better," I offered, "but we both know I'll just be eavesdropping anyway."

And we both knew there were very few things she'd be unwilling to tell me, so if she wanted privacy it meant stirring up no small amount of curiosity from me.

"Fine," she gave in with surprisingly little protest and returned her focus to Arya who waited for her to finish what sounded like a one-sided conversation expectantly. That was the other reason I liked little WD, she never batted an eye at my interactions with Willow which meant I got to speak freely without only getting silence in return.

"I'm waiting," the cherry red-haired wolf said with a grin, "And if the details are juicy, kindly keep it PG for my innocent ears."

Both Willow and I scoffed at that. There was nothing PG about her or her ears.

"Nothing juicy," Willow assured her, "I didn't get enough information from him in the bar. I had questions that needed answers, and you know once I set my mind on something I won't be able to rest until it's taken care of."

We both stared at her waiting.

"And?" Arya drew out the one-word question.

"And nothing. I went there, I asked him about the pack, he answered, and I decided I would help him. There's nothing else to tell."

Willow sounded entirely unbothered about the entire thing, as if having a pre-sunrise rendezvous with a former friend turned betrayer was an everyday occurrence. She sounded so unbothered, that even I might've believed her if not for the teeth lightly tugging at the corner of her lips.

"So Rory says he needs help, and you say yes sir, let me go on a road trip with you where we will be stuck together night and day rekindling what we once were as we work together to solve the pack mystery and clear my name in the process?"

Arya asked dryly, "What is this, a poorly plotted rom com or something? Do you really think this is a good choice for you —that *he's* a good choice for you?"

I certainly didn't.

"I'm not choosing him," Willow said, walking to the bed to fold the jeans I'd left atop it and adding them to her bag, "I'm choosing to be the bigger person and go help someone who needs it. My history with Rory has nothing to do with it."

"I'm not buying it." Arya turned to where I presume she thought I was sitting—she was a foot or so off—and asked, "What about you, Theo?"

"Not even a little bit," I deadpanned. I would've believed her more had she said she was going with him so she could dispose of his body in a swamp along the route between packs as revenge or even if she'd simply said she wanted closure with a former friend.

"He believes me," Willow fibbed.

"Liar." I smiled at the contradiction. "There's no way he's not on my side here, so what is it really? Do you just want to go back and show them that they were wrong about you? Do you miss your parents? Or is it Rory that you missed, and now that he's back in your life, you're finding it a little bit challenging to let go?"

If it were possible, my face would've drained of color as a flush of red rose to Willow's cheeks.

So it was him.

"It's not him," she protested, "I don't feel that way about him, I just—" She broke off and I wondered if I even wanted her to continue speaking or if it were better to stay in the realm of things unknown.

"It's just what?" I guess WD didn't feel the same.

"I just feel like I need to go with him, okay? I'm allowed to follow my feelings sometimes without justifying them to you." She looked from Arya to me and added, "Or you."

"I didn't say anything," I said with raised hands.

"You didn't have to." Usually that was a connection I treasured. Currently it felt like a curse.

"You feel drawn to him, then?" Arya asked, not to be deterred, "Drawn to him like you'd feel drawn to your mate?"

For the first time in my existence, I was thankful I couldn't eat. If I could, that cinnamon roll from earlier would've been making a reappearance across Willow's bedspread right about now.

"I have no interest in becoming his mate, and he has no interest in that either," she said, but I wondered if any of us really believed it.

I'd seen the way the Alpha looked at her in the bar. She may not have realized what that gleam in his eye was, but I did. It was the sign of a man realizing what he wants and deciding to go for it.

"Even if it's fated?" If I didn't know better I'd think Arya was deliberately trying to re-kill me.

"Rory is not my fated mate."

"Damn right he isn't," I grumbled.

"He might be," Arya argued, "It could be why you feel

like you need to go with him—why you were so close as kids."

"I would know by now if Rory and I were fated." Willow dismissed the idea like I'd dismiss a suggestion on how to properly haunt a house. "I'm pretty sure if I have a fated mate they were hit by a train, and I'll have to wait for my next lifetime to meet them."

"Or they were cursed by a witch," I offered helpfully. All I earned was a glare in return. Rude. "What? It happens!"

"Look I'm not on team Rory, okay? I hope he steps on a thousand legos and never has the right amount of wrapping paper left when he wraps a present." A fair hex if I'd ever heard one. "I just think maybe you should be open to it— otherwise you'll never know. Maybe after a good amount of groveling you two could find a way to be happy together. You could finally go home, *if* that's what you want."

It better freaking not be. I wasn't sure how Willow would feel about being bound in rope and brainwashed, but I wasn't against finding out if that was the only way I could get her to stay.

"I don't." Willow's declaration left no room to question it and thankfully wasn't accompanied by a lip bite. Good. No need for the rope then. "I don't want to go home, okay? I like my life here. I'm going back because it's the right thing to do. As for Rory, we aren't—we just— he just—"

"He just what?" Arya and I asked in unison as the crunch of tires rolling up came from outside.

"He just arrived."

CHAPTER 6

Willow

Arya may have thought I should be open to whatever may or may not develop with Rory—heavy on the *not*—but that didn't stop her from standing on the porch, arms crossed and hip popped, glaring at him from the moment he got out of his car.

"I take it she isn't a fan of mine," he observed as he shut the covered compartment at the base of the truck bed with a click. I refused to be moved by the fact he'd carried it from the house and loaded it into the car without me saying a word. Except maybe I had been the tiniest bit impressed by it.

I really needed to have higher standards when it came to what qualified for swooning, but my body was easily swayed by acts of service—or at the very least my hormones seemed to be. There was just something about a man doing something for you as if you were entitled to it without having to ask that got me every time. So even though I meant it when I said I wasn't interested in him, I'd be lying if I said he wasn't a smidge hotter in that moment.

And yet, when I glanced back at the porch to the translucent figure leaning in the doorway behind Arya, I knew that the hint of attraction I felt toward Rory was nothing compared to the feelings I had for Theo—the ones I tried to keep from rearing their head because there was nowhere for them to go.

But damnit there was a cinnamon roll waiting for me on the kitchen table this morning that was currently in a to go bag on the passenger seat reminding me. Who wouldn't be swayed by something like that, let alone the million other things he did for me on a daily basis? So really, my body heating up at Rory carrying a suitcase Theo had more or less packed for me was practically a betrayal. It didn't make sense.

Unless Arya was right about us being fated, of course. Then it would make perfect sense.

"Low?" Rory's hand was warm as it rested on my shoulder, "You good?"

"Yeah," I said, pulling myself from that pointless line of thinking as I tried to remember what he'd said to me. "Did you ask me something before?"

His eyes searched between mine before shaking his head. "No, at least nothing important."

"Right, okay then." I kicked at the dirt at my feet and added, "I'm just going to say bye to them, and then I'm good to head out."

"Them?" he asked. If I wasn't mistaken his face turned a fraction paler.

"Them," I said, gesturing to the porch. "Arya and Theo. It'll only take a minute."

"Take your time." He eyed the porch warily before sliding into the driver's seat and shutting the car door behind him.

His reaction wasn't wholly unexpected—most people weren't a fan of ghosts in my limited experience. I had only explained Theo's presence to a handful of friends, and even then it was usually because he did something to force me to explain the unexplainable. Things like the couch levitating while Beckett was sitting on it.

He was, understandably, less than thrilled to suddenly become airborne and had been wary of Theo ever since. Arya, on the other hand, had embraced my ghostly roommate from their first encounter. Rather than be put off by the floating baked goods and self-mixing whisk she stumbled upon in the kitchen, she made a list of treats she'd like to request be added to the rotation.

I think she was secretly his favorite, but she was definitely the exception that proved the rule. Most people in the pack did—and would—react like Rory and be wary of any paranormal activity. Which was honestly a bit hypocritical considering we changed into wolves on a semi-regular basis and it didn't get much farther from normal than that. You'd think a ghost would be nothing, but instead people kept their distance as if one would suddenly decide to follow them home.

Maybe I should've invited Theo to come back to Thornbridge with me. Despite Rory's assurances I wouldn't be disturbed, I couldn't help but wonder how many of my former pack mates would risk upsetting the Alpha to get in a jab or two at the murderous girl who cried wolf–or at least suspicious supernatural abduction.

It would be far more than wishful thinking to hope my parents would try to break the Alpha's decree for any other reason. Reasons like they missed me. Reasons like they regretted letting the pack drive me away—for driving me away themselves.

I didn't need them, anyway. I had my true pack. I had my home. I had Arya. I had Skye. I had Theo. Who had time to mourn disloyal losses when there was such love to be had?

"Call me when you get there," Arya said with a pout before wrapping her arms around me and whispering in my ear, "And remember to try to be open to whatever may or may not happen."

I pulled away ready to roll my eyes but laughed instead when she added, "But also remember our code word for body disposal is 'I need a bath token.'"

"I know the code, but I don't think it'll be necessary. They already think I hid one body, probably best not to add fuel to the fire and actually hide a second."

She shrugged and said, "As long as you remember it. No judgment from me if it's needed or not."

I wasn't sure if I should be touched or terrified that she seemed to mean it.

"I'm also happy to help with disposal of anything—be it an entire body or simply certain parts of it," Theo offered with a smile, "It'll be like it never existed."

"And how will you pull that off?"

He waggled his eyebrows as I walked toward him and said, "Don't you worry, I have my ways. Probably best that you don't know the details. They'd bore you anyway."

"Plausible deniability," I said in a mock serious tone, "I like it."

What I didn't like was the somber look in his eye like he was looking at me for the last time in our—well, my life instead of saying goodbye for a few days.

"You've got Skye covered while I'm gone?" Was all I could think to say to fill the ever-thickening silence between us. "If not I can ask Arya or Beck to swing by and pick her up."

"Yeah I have our girl covered. No need to enlist my bestie or WD." I refused to melt at him referring to Skye as *our* girl. It felt too risky—too fragile. We were in this house tip-toeing around the fact that we were building a life together that couldn't be a full life, from household chores, sharing dreams, and taking care of our giant fluff ball. Theo was the one person I wanted to grow old with and the one person who could never grow old.

And what exactly was I supposed to do with that?

Maybe Arya was right. Maybe I needed to start being more open to other possibilities that presented themselves to me. Opportunities like Rory. He'd stayed in the car during my goodbyes, but he had rolled down his window, no doubt listening in.

My feelings for him had been the emotion of a young girl —I knew that now. They weren't built on going through trials together. They didn't grow each time a small act of consideration affirmed a long-lasting trust that was built one stone at a time. They didn't make me feel like I could let out my crazy and all he'd do was smile wider. They weren't unconditional.

They weren't what I'd built with a ghost, but maybe they didn't need to be. Maybe they'd grow with time—if that's even what he wanted. He certainly hadn't before, maybe it was silly of me to even be going down this line of thinking now. At worst it was setting myself up for heartbreak, and at best it was a waste of time better spent focused on helping a former friend.

I blamed Arya.

"I'll see you soon then," I assured both Theo and myself. I was coming back—no matter what, I was coming back.

"Yes you will." I felt the chill of his hand brush over my cheek. We both pretended I didn't shiver. The steel in his voice may have been a promise or a threat, but whatever it was, it sent a wave of warmth through my body—whether I wanted it to or not.

With nothing left to say I gave him a final nod, hugged Arya one more time, and walked down the porch steps to the passenger side of Rory's truck—the same truck I'd spent countless hours in as a teenager.

"Ready?" he asked.

Not even a little bit.

"Of course, let's get going." I kept an eye on the porch through the side view mirror as we went farther and farther away from home.

Theo didn't leave the porch. He was still there, watching me, until it was too far away for me to see.

"WE COULD PLAY THE LICENSE PLATE GAME," RORY suggested for what felt like the tenth time.

"No thanks." It wasn't like we were going to find more than two states anyway. We'd been driving for a little more than three hours and had seen maybe twenty cars in that time. Why he was taking the back roads instead of the interstate was beyond me, but I refused to be accused of passenger seat driving again. I kept my mouth shut.

"Want to play I spy instead?"

"You know I would," I said snapping my fingers, "but don't you know, I think we'd run out of ideas real quick once we got through the trees, snow, and road, don't you?"

By now the world was one-quarter snow, and three-quarters grey mush outside and neither would make for a particularly riveting game. It wasn't frigid enough during the day for it to fall and stick, but the temperature still dropped throughout the night.

"Just trying to fill the time," he said patiently. The radio had turned into static thirty minutes ago. It always did when we were this deep into the mountains. Unsurprisingly, his old truck didn't have a way to connect to our phones, and though I'd considered it, it would be too rude to put in my headphones and listen to my audiobook.

"Why didn't you fly with the others, anyway?" The other

men from the bachelor party had bragged about the charter plane they'd gotten for the bachelor party half the night. "Even with all of those fools it had to be more comfortable than a seven hour drive."

A seven hour drive that was going to be more like eight or nine at the pace he was going. Honestly, what had happened to the boy who considered speed limits a sign of oppression?

"I wasn't sure when I'd be coming back." He shifted in his seat and cleared his throat. "Seemed best to drive myself just in case."

Just in case convincing me to speak to him took more than a couple days. Just in case I decided to come back with him.

"It's a good thing neither of us get car sick then." Because apparently talking about puke was the best response I could put together.

I mean, what were we supposed to talk about? Should I say hey, remember that one time I asked you to trust me and you literally turned your back and walked away while everyone I knew and loved hurled insults and accusations at me? It was a bit too early in our time trapped together to risk those kinds of conversations, but I didn't know how to talk about anything else until we did. Or maybe we would just continue not to speak at all. Silence may be best for survival—both his and mine.

One wrong word and my wolf would be ready to tear out his throat. I wasn't stupid, I know his could subdue her, but she was fast and he was preoccupied while driving. She hadn't settled since we'd gotten into his truck this morning, but she'd at least stopped growling inside of me. Even if I found a way to forgive Rory for his betrayal, I was more than skeptical she ever would—fated or not fated.

"We could play two truths and a lie." Rory sounded far too nonchalant for that to actually be a casual suggestion.

"You think we should play a game where we guess truths and lies?" I asked dryly, "Seriously?"

He rolled his lips between his teeth and muttered, "Yeah, maybe not my best plan."

"No," I agreed, "Not your best plan."

"We could talk about the weather, I guess?" he said a few minutes later, "It's been a little bit warm for February, don't you think? I personally love winter—"

"Since when?" I asked incredulously, "I seem to recall having to drag you—literally drag you—out of your bed whenever it snowed because you were so sensitive to the chill you refused to get up on your own."

"Are you sure you're remembering that correctly?" he asked as he glanced at me across the bench seat of the truck, "I don't think that was me. Maybe you're thinking of someone else. Memories do start to fade as we get older. It's okay if yours isn't what it used to be."

"Are you freaking kidding me? Your mother used to call me begging me to walk across the street to come and get you when she'd given up."

As a brilliant smile stretched across his face I realized that yes, he was, in fact, kidding around with me.

"Did you ever consider that maybe it was less about the

cold and more that I just liked waking up to you in my bed in the mornings?"

My mouth fell open but words failed me.

"I'm sorry," I managed to say after about thirty seconds of being gobsmacked, "I think I just misheard you, what did you say?"

"You heard exactly what I just said." There wasn't an ounce of shame in his voice when he added, "And if you think I didn't mean every word of it, I'll tell you right now that you're wrong."

What the actual fuck was happening, and how could he possibly be so calm about it?

"I think you had a brain transplant while I was gone," I said under my breath.

"No brain transplant needed," he chuckled, "Just a new perspective on the same thoughts."

I wasn't unpacking that trapped in a car with him for the rest of the day. I'd keep it neatly wrapped in a dark corner of my mind, secured with zip ties and duct tape.

Rather than stare at him from the passenger seat, I turned to look out the window at the trees passing by. Trees were safer. Trees weren't sitting with a ray of sunlight illuminating them from the window as they drove with one hand resting on the steering wheel and the other draped across the seat behind me. Trees didn't have a self-satisfied smirk on their faces that was equal parts infuriating and intriguing.

But just because I wasn't looking at him didn't mean I wasn't fully aware of every move he made, from the drumming of his fingers on the seat back to the shifting of his leg as he adjusted his speed. It would be impossible to think he was anything but a pack Alpha. Even doing something as simple as driving down a road, he projected that sense of security, of control I couldn't help be drawn to in any setting, let alone when he was sitting two feet away.

Forced proximity really was a bitch.

"So are we still not playing two truths and a lie then, because I love that game?" I jumped a full three inches in my seat at the new voice beside me, causing Rory to swerve into the other lane for a moment before righting the wheel.

"What the hell was that for?" he asked, but he wasn't the male I was addressing.

"Theo!" I yelled, "You can't just pop into a moving vehicle and act like it's normal. What are you even doing here?"

And why did his presence make me feel like I'd been caught doing something I shouldn't?

"Your ghost is in here?" Rory asked, goosebumps already appearing on his arms from the chill in the air.

"You were taking too long to call me," Theo said with a shrug, "So I decided it would be best for us all if I just went ahead and showed up."

"Wha— What about Skye?" I sputtered. I don't know why I was looking for reasons for him to leave other than every inch of me wanted him to stay. Then again, every inch of me also hated the idea of being trapped with not one, but two men I shouldn't want in the cab of a truck.

"I asked Arya to watch her, obviously." His side-eye would have even made a teenager do a double take. "Like I'd leave our dog with no one to care for her while I gallivant with you across the country."

"It's two states away."

"Exactly," he said.

"And how exactly did you ask Arya? Do you have some kind of mind-speak powers you've never told me about?" And who else was he using them on? A small spike of envy shot through me at the thought.

"Don't be ridiculous." Because that would be the most ridiculous thing about this conversation. "I wrote her a note on her bathroom mirror so she'd see it when she took a shower after hitting the gym."

"You what?"

"It felt like the best choice at the time." He paused and seemed to consider it further. "Except I guess I should've removed any tripping hazards. I didn't expect her to jump like that. I feel a little bad about her ankle, but hopefully Beck can use this as his chance to be a knight in shining armor."

I shook my head because really, what else was there to do.

"Your train of thought really concerns me sometimes."

"I like to keep you on your toes. It's how I make sure you're never bored." He smiled my favorite boyish grin. "Feel free to thank me anytime."

"Thank you, your highness," I said as insincerely as I could manage without breaking into my own grin, "For ensuring I never have a moment's peace."

"You're welcome, darling." He placed a hand to his chest. "It's truly my privilege and pleasure."

The snort that left me was far from ladylike, but it couldn't be helped. I was still half-chuckling to myself when Rory leaned his head too far forward to glance between me and the seat between us.

"So," he drew out the word, "Your ghost will be joining us, I take it?"

"More like he's joining us in *our* adventure," Theo muttered, "Or at least chauffeuring us. Maybe he'll let me get him one of those little hats drivers wear in the movies."

"Yes," I said back to Rory, trying not to picture him in a chauffeur's cap. Unfortunately the image did nothing to make him any less attractive. "Theo will be joining us."

"Great." Though he made it sound like it was anything but. "Road trip with a ghost. What could go wrong?"

For me, I thought, looking between them, quite a lot.

CHAPTER 7

Willow

"If he zaps me one more time, I swear to god I will find an exorcist to remove him from this plane of existence and send him on to the next."

Rory's knuckles were white where he gripped the steering wheel. I had some serious concerns he would break it. We still had at least another thirty minutes to go until we reached the Thornbridge Pack territory, and I really didn't want to call someone to come get us. My nerves were high enough just passing through the familiar landscaping, I didn't need a surprise reunion with one of the pack members on top of it.

"I don't see what he's complaining about," Theo defended, "I'm helping him stay awake at the wheel, he could be a little more grateful."

"I think he'd be more grateful if you would agree to keep your phantom hands to yourself."

Half of his mouth drew up in what could only be described as a devilish smirk.

"If that's really what you want, darling then I guess I can oblige." He looked straight ahead and added the caveat, "at least for now."

"He'll stop," I said more as an order to Theo than an assurance to Rory. The Alpha grumbled something unintelligible I took as acceptance and went back to focusing on the road.

It had been a long, long drive. Theo was always a bit mischievous. I imagined anyone would be after I didn't even know how many years of wandering the world as a spirit all alone–I suspected he wasn't too much older than me, but couldn't be sure. Unfortunately for Rory, he'd taken his antics to another level on this trip.

When Rory would leave the truck, be it to grab food or fill up the tank he'd come back to a locked door and an icy handle he'd have to thaw to get through. Eventually he started entering through the passenger side and sliding over to the driver seat.

Whenever he tried to start a conversation with me, Theo would inevitably provide so much commentary I'd end up not understanding a word Rory said or cracking up at the most inopportune times due to whatever quip or absurdity left my ghost's mouth.

I should feel worse for the Alpha than I did, but I'd rather spend hours laughing than hours unpacking whatever tension laid between us—between *all* of us. Plus there really was little that could stop Theo from doing what he wanted, especially once he knew I thought it may be the tiniest bit funny.

When we turned down a winding gravel road I knew we would be pulling through the pack compound's gates only moments later. To the humans passing by it probably looked like a run down, abandoned summer camp in the woods, but I knew differently. Every inch of the fence surrounding the perimeter was reinforced and the compound had been anything but rustic.

A derelict plot of land in the woods was simply far easier to hide from the humans than a set of mansion-like log cabins with a strip of businesses, library, and school to boot in the middle of the woods. If they knew what was really hidden, there would be tourists, and as every shifter and service industry worker knew, tourists were the ticket to hell —or, at the very least, the ticket to discovery.

"Are we driving into a cult? Is that what this is?" Theo asked, his nose wrinkled in distaste, "Because if he's recruiting you to be his co-leader or hoping to turn you into his fiftieth wife, just know I am happy to zap anyone that needs zapping on your behalf."

"Wait two minutes and then we can revisit that thought." We were cresting the small hill at the front of the property now. Coming into view in the distance was a too familiar yet different version of what used to be my home. When Theo saw it, his breath caught.

"It's bigger than I remembered," I admitted, "But I guess the plan always was to continue growing."

"Most things have," Rory acknowledged, "but we still have a ways to go. There's always room to grow."

But how much growth was really needed? I was all for

progress, but I couldn't help but wonder what was lost with the expansion. The Sun Meadow Pack was more or less a small town, and every pack member knew each other—looked after one another. How could the Thornbridge Pack accomplish that with the population of a small city?

"I guess a lot has changed in eight years," I said dryly.

"A lot hasn't." Rory's eyes bore into mine for a second longer than they should have while operating a motor vehicle—even with the instincts of an Alpha.

"I promise you more does, buddy." Theo's response had my lip twitching just as Rory looked away with a grin of his own I couldn't quite interpret.

I didn't even have time to try, because when I looked back at the road in front of us, we were pulling into the city.

And that's when I started seeing the faces that felt like knives lodged in my heart—knives that had stabbed me in the back to reach it.

There was my high school English teacher who'd once told me I was one of a kind, only to call me a murderer a few months later.

There was a man who'd graduated with me, now holding hands with a woman I recognized from the class a few years ahead of us. She held a baby on her hip, and a young boy walked beside them on the sidewalk. If I hadn't been driven out, would it have been me with a pup on my hip?

We passed more and more faces, some familiar and some new, but they all had one thing in common: they were staring at us. Some stared with open mouths. Some immediately turned to the person next to them to comment. Some just turned pale. Those ones I always recognized. It took all of my self-control, or maybe it was self-preservation, not to give a little wave.

I was back, bitches, and not a single one of us was happy about it.

"Welcome home." Correction, none of us were happy about it, except maybe Rory. His face grew more and more joyful the farther we got into town.

"This isn't my home," I reminded him.

He simply shrugged.

"Maybe it doesn't feel like it," he said, "but this is always going to be your home, Low. It was once. It could be again if you wanted it to be."

"She doesn't." If Rory could've heard Theo's tone he'd have surely rethought what he said next.

As he pulled into a driveway in front of a large white house with a wraparound porch he parked the truck, turned to me, and said, "I'm really hoping by the end of this that you want it to be, because if I know one thing in life, it's that watching you walk away is the greatest regret that will haunt me for the rest of it."

I was saved from having to think of a coherent response to that by a rapping of knuckles on the driver side window. As Rory broke the tractor beam gaze he'd somehow trapped me in to get out of the truck I vowed to say a blessing for my savior—vow not to speak to any pack mates be damned.

"Was that line supposed to be swoon-worthy?" Theo asked with an unimpressed look, "Because I really don't see it."

"Let's just forget that happened," I suggested and reached for the door handle.

"Fine by me."

As I stepped out of the truck and shut the door behind me, I briefly considered hopping right back in when my brain registered whose voice was speaking to Rory on the other side. Fuck my life. I hadn't even gotten my bag from the truck bed, and the asshole had already found me.

"I just don't get why you'd bring her here, the whole damn pack is already talking about it, and you've only been here for the five minutes it took to drive through town to your house," Miles complained. I decided I would not, in fact, say a blessing for him after all. "If you had to bring her, why didn't you at least try to be discreet about it? You know this is going to cause issues, she's a damn murderer."

"Not yet," I smiled as I came around the front of the truck, "But I'm getting closer to becoming one by the second."

His lip curled as he looked at me the way I'd look at an olive or spam.

"Willow," my name was like a curse leaving his mouth, "Here I was hoping you'd found a way to disappear for good. Back to get more blood on your hands? Hoping to cause more pain? Maybe ruin another family?"

"Only if it's yours," I said cheerfully, "Prey on any unsuspecting females lately? Are you still sticking to stalking, or have you escalated to some light breaking and entering now to get a better view when they sleep?"

"Maybe I should sneak into his room tonight," Theo said

from his spot sitting on the front of the truck. "I've never tried planting images or dreams in someone's mind while they sleep, but I bet there's a way to do it. Maybe if I just whisper thoughts of his own demise in his ear it'll stick. Or maybe I can move things around his room, make him think it's haunted and then when he tells everyone else no one will believe him."

Personally, I loved that idea, but now wasn't the time for talking to ghosts the others couldn't see. I didn't need to give Miles anything else to use as ammunition against me in the pack. The short visit would be unpleasant enough as it was.

"Okay let's all just take a breath, shall we?" Rory walked between Miles and I with a hand raised in either direction, "Low, you know he's not a stalker, and Miles, we still can't be sure what happened in those woods. No one has been able to prove Faye was killed in a challenge."

I wanted to say that I did, in fact, know Miles was a stalker, but the words caught in my throat at the latter half of Rory's statement.

"You don't know?" I asked, my voice somewhere between speaking and a whisper.

It wasn't hurt that ran through my veins—I'd buried those emotions years ago. It was fury. I took a step toward him until my pointed finger dug into his stupidly hard chest, cursing him for being built like a slab of concrete. Inside me, my wolf longed to break through my skin and tear at both the man who'd caused our friend such harm and the man who'd stood by and let him. The man who still questioned me.

"You show up in my town, in my pack," I said through gritted teeth, driving my finger into him with each statement, "You disrupt my life, asking for my help. You drive me back to this place with these godforsaken people I'd happily never see again, because you say you need me, but you can't be sure if there was a challenge? If you don't believe me, what the hell am I even doing here, Rory?"

His eyes grew wider than a full moon, and he didn't take a step away—no Alpha would give up ground to an attacker—but he did move his hands until they were lifted in front of him in surrender.

"That's not what I said," he defended, "You're putting words in my mouth."

"Then maybe you should've kept it shut so nothing could get in there."

"Who the hell do you think you are talking to the Alpha like that?"

Miles growled the question as he crowded me from the side. If he were a little taller, or the boots of my heels were a little shorter, I imagined he thought he was towering over me. If he thought that was intimidating, he was stupider than I thought.

"He isn't my Alpha," I said, not bothering to look away from Rory, "And I'll remind you that you're not a physical threat to me, Miles, so back up before someone makes you."

Rory looked at me with a plea in his eyes to be the bigger person and let this go. It was the same plea I saw when we were kids. The same plea I'd always given into before, but not anymore. I wasn't going to let some second rate stalker wannabe Alpha male intimidate me.

And neither, it seemed, would Theo.

Miles' biggest mistake was his undoing, because the moment he reached out to grab me by the upper arm, he was flung five feet back with a jolt so powerful it sent a crackling sound in the air.

"Can we go home now?" My ghost asked as he hopped from the truck to stand beside me. The chill of his aura helped calm the fury threatening to burn me from the inside out. "We really should've driven separately."

"We'll just fly back," I told him, then paused and asked, "You can go on a plane, right? We've never tested it."

"I'm sure it'll be fine." He shrugged his shoulders and rested one of his arms atop of mine. "I can always meet you back there. Travel is pretty quick when you can wink in and out of existence."

And yet he'd chosen to sit in a cramped truck cab with me on the journey here.

"You're not getting on a plane." Rory's eyes narrowed as he spoke, "We've been on the road for hours, and I think we'll all be more agreeable after we get some rest."

He rounded the truck to pull our bags from the bed, carrying one under each arm as he nodded toward the house.

"Just stay tonight. At the very least we can look at the spot I mentioned to you tomorrow. I know you're curious or you wouldn't have agreed to come in the first place."

He was, annoying as it was, not wrong. I did want to

know what the heck was going on that the signs and that damn red cloak were popping up again after all of this time.

"I'll stay tonight." His lips curved in a smile that was too self-assured for my liking. I stared up at the big white house and asked, "Is this the place?"

Rory's cheeks turned a half shade warmer as he nodded, "Yeah this is where you'll be staying."

"She's staying in your house?" A disgruntled, still flat on his back Miles complained, "And you really think that's not going to cause problems in the pack?"

"And you really think as his Beta you have any right to question him? Didn't you just give me shit for that five seconds ago when I'm not even in this pack?" Freaking hypocrite. I turned on Rory whose grin stretched from ear to ear, but it dropped when I said, "And you, what does he mean your house? I'm not staying with you."

"Yes, you are." That was his full retort before turning on his heel and marching up the steps with our bags.

"Why?" I marched right after him. I wasn't going to be steamrolled by him. I wasn't his follower anymore. "Did you decide to get rid of the guest houses? Because last time I checked, I qualified as a guest."

He balanced one of the bags under his arm as he keyed in a code to the red front door before pushing it open and stepping inside. "You really want to stay in a guest house alone once the pack knows you're back?"

He had a point.

"Are you saying your pack will attack me unprovoked?"

He dropped the bags and turned to me.

"Are you saying you think none of them would come up with justification enough to claim provocation?"

I hated when he was right.

"I can think of more than one justification right now," came Miles' grumbling from the porch. I guess he'd found the strength to stand again. What a pity.

At my silence, Rory stepped closer until our toes were nearly touching, hands planted on his tapered hips. Unlike Miles, he didn't have to try to tower over me. It happened naturally.

"Would you rather I call your parents and see if you can stay with them?" He raised one eyebrow and looked far too pleased by the growl that escaped me.

Fine. I stepped around him and grabbed my bag, walking toward the staircase across the entryway, "So which room is mine?"

He caught up to me easily and took the bag from my hands as he fell into step beside me. His unused hand at my back as he guided me up the stairs and brought me to a door at the end of a long hall.

"You can stay in this room for now," he opened the door and gestured for me to step through, "My room is right across the hall."

"Of course it is," Theo grumbled. What did it say about my current state that I hadn't noticed him following us until just then?

"What do you mean by 'for now?'" I asked the Alpha leaning in the doorway, "Are we going somewhere else?"

Rory pushed off from the spot against the door jam,

strode over to me, and tucked a strand of hair behind my ear. The warmth from his hand was such a change from the cold I'd grown accustomed to when Theo performed the same action.

"I'm hoping one of us will be." He gave me a crooked smile and turned to leave, calling without looking back, "I'll let you get settled. Come downstairs when you're ready for dinner."

"Hopefully you're not on the menu." The humor in Theo's words failed to reach his eyes.

CHAPTER 8

Theo

Whatever this hometown reunion thing that was happening here was, I didn't like it. Not liking it was expected. I was fine with not liking it. What had me more concerned was I couldn't tell if Willow did.

Sure, she was angry at the Alpha and Beta outside, but I'd seen her soften on our way to the pack compound. I'd seen her do it again at dinner.

Sometimes I liked to watch her when she didn't know I was there—not during times I shouldn't of course. I'd never take advantage of her, but checking on her now and again without fully appearing helped me make sure the smile she wore each day was real instead of a mask for the benefit of others. I wanted to know how she really felt, not how she wanted me to think she felt. So if that meant the occasional moment of spying, that was a price I was willing to pay.

I let her think I wasn't at dinner as she sat across from

Rory at his dining room table. He made her steak, green beans, and mashed potatoes.

I hated him a little for knowing that was her favorite.

I hated him a little less when her nose wrinkled slightly at her first bite of mashed potatoes. I guess mine were better.

Watching Willow with Rory was half wondering if she'd throw her knife into his eye from across the table or if she was on a vacation with her best friend. When he asked if she wanted to go on a run with his wolf after the meal my heart would've stopped had it still been capable of beating. If she'd said yes I think I would've died a second death, or at the very least caused his first.

But even if she didn't agree to prance with him in the moonlight I watched the way she smiled when he said something I'm sure he found funny. I saw the way her eyes softened when he spoke about how emotional he'd been when his father transferred the Alpha title to him a year ago. The former Alpha and his mate had apparently gone on an extended trip after the transition to avoid any uncomfortable tensions accompanying the change in power.

I didn't like the way she sighed when he talked about the weekend cookout they still had with former friends and family each week or the giggle that escaped her when they recalled getting the run down hunk of metal he called a truck stuck in a ditch on the way to a concert. Apparently they'd missed the concert but danced on the side of the road to the cd playing in the truck cab.

How adorable, just like a toddler screeching in a food court.

And now she was sitting there, a mug of tea that I didn't make her cradled in her hands as she curled up in an over-sized armchair by the fire Rory had built for her. Whatever anger she'd shown toward him in the driveway had already dissipated.

"Will you take me where you saw the cloak tomorrow?" she asked him. "I want to see if my wolf can find anything to track. It's a long shot that anything's lingering from when you saw them, but maybe they returned while you were gone."

"Are you doubting my tracking ability?" the Alpha asked, almost amused by the idea of it.

"I'm not doubting yours," she clarified, "I'm just confident in my own. Come on, Rory. You may be the stronger wolf, but we both know I'm the better tracker."

"Maybe," he relented and took a sip from his own mug where he sat on the couch with an ankle over his knee.

"Definitely," she corrected. My girl was nothing if not confident in her abilities, and why shouldn't she be? A male who was intimidated by the talent of a female was the purest form of pathetic. I begrudgingly gave Rory a speck of credit for not insisting his skill outmatched hers.

I kept my distance as they continued to speak, and the happier she looked the more hollow my chest became.

This was wrong. All of it was wrong.

She shouldn't be in the Alpha's home, she should be in ours, curled up on the couch with Skye on one side and me on the other. She should be wrapped in the woefully knitted blanket Arya attempted to make her for Christmas last year, and it should be the chamomile tea blend I made for her cradled between her hands. It should be me she smiled at over her cup.

But it wasn't.

Eventually, it couldn't be, and I knew that. I'd have to watch her smile at someone else eventually, to fall in love and build a life with someone eventually, and I knew that too.

I just hoped eventually hadn't already come and gone right under my nose.

CHAPTER 9

Willow

I needed Rory to trust me if I was going to get to the bottom of what was happening in the pack. That was the conclusion I'd come to last night after he'd left me in my room. So despite the frustration I felt after the encounter with Miles, the confusion brewing in my head from his parting comment, and the growing conflict in my gut each time I looked between Rory's warm eyes and Theo's translucent ones, I went down to dinner, and I played pretend.

I pretended I was still the girl Rory had grown up with. I pretended I wasn't hanging onto every scrap of information about the pack that may explain recent events or get me closer to finding the person wearing the red cloak.

And eventually, as the night grew darker and the fire grew brighter, I pretended that I was still pretending.

It was easier than it should've been to slip back into old habits of hanging on every word that left Rory's mouth all while giving him just enough flack to keep him on his toes. I'd have followed him off a cliff when we were younger, but I also would've forced him to bring us both parachutes so we survived the fall.

And now we were here, in his kitchen as he plated our food while we waited for the coffee pot to finish brewing, and it felt like a dreamscape someone had pulled me into based on my teenage wishes that hadn't come true.

Is this what we would've been doing the entire time we'd been apart if Faye had never disappeared? Would he have waited another year after graduation to ask me on a date? Maybe we would've done something neither of us were talented at like ice skating or maybe we'd have revisited the arcade we loved as kids.

Maybe we would still be just friends. Maybe we'd be mated.

We'd never know for sure. It was pointless to speculate, and yet my mind continued running rampant with what ifs and maybes. I loved the life I'd built. I loved my pack, my friends, and I loved—

No.

That would only lead to heartbreak. I wouldn't even think the words. I loved my life and the people in it, but there was a comfort a sense of being known—that came with being next to someone who'd known you at every stage of your life that felt like a warm hug on a cold winter's day.

So I kept pretending to pretend, because admitting to anything else was too risky. It was too late to entertain the maybes.

"Eat up." Rory slid the plate of hash browns, eggs, and bacon in front of me along with a mug full of coffee that, based on the color, was exactly the way I liked it.

"Thanks." I muttered, taking my first sip. It was good, but I'd been wrong. It wasn't exactly the way I liked, but it was close. Theo would've gotten it perfect, but he'd also been making it for me for years. Practice truly had made perfect.

"Oh, I almost forgot." Rory popped into the pantry and returned with a small glass bottle a moment later. "I still don't get how you eat this, but whatever makes you happy."

"Don't knock it until you try it." I added a tiny drizzle of maple syrup to the crispy bacon on my plate with a smile. "Salty and sweet is always the answer."

I took a bite and hummed in satisfaction to prove my point.

"I'll take your word for it."

I took another bite and said, "Your loss."

Rory grabbed his own mug and plate before sliding onto the bar stool beside mine at the counter. We ate in silence for a few minutes, and I was grateful for the light music he'd turned on when he'd started cooking to fill the space between us. It helped calm my wolf who hadn't quite forgiven him yet for his betrayal.

I meant it when I told Arya I didn't believe that Rory was my fated mate, but my wolf had all but claimed him as our chosen mate before we'd left. She'd felt safe with him, and that safety had been cruelly ripped away.

She wasn't the type to give second chances. If I was being honest, I usually wasn't either. The only reason she was tolerating his presence was her loyalty to Faye and concern for Emma. If history was repeating itself, then a threat was undoubtedly closing in on the girl, I just needed to confirm what that threat was.

When we'd each cleared our plates and finished our coffee, Rory stood to rinse his and set them in the dishwasher. Before I stood to do the same, the dining ware floated toward the sink without me lifting a finger.

"Your ghost I presume?" Rory sounded the opposite of impressed, whereas I felt positively giddy. I couldn't even see where Theo was and still he was taking care of me. I was more than a little smug to have the Alpha see it.

"He's a good one," I said and hopped off my stool, "Give me five minutes to change and then I'm ready to head out if you are."

He agreed then mumbled under his breath, "It's like he's her freaking maid."

"Just a gentleman, actually," I called back.

"Yeah, dipshit," Theo's voice came from somewhere in the living room, "I'm a gentleman."

Sometimes I really wish he wasn't, even if I knew nothing could ever truly come of it. Maybe then there wouldn't be room for thoughts of Rory at all.

"I KNOW WHAT YOU'RE DOING," I SAID FROM THE passenger seat, "and it's not going to work."

"I don't know what you're talking about." I would've

believed him if I hadn't heard him use that innocently sweet tone to get out of trouble a thousand times when we were growing up. I'd never quite mastered it myself.

"I'm not going to speak to them, and I don't want to see them." And he couldn't make me even if he tried. Alphas rarely used their bark on pack mates to force compliance—the whole taking away free will thing was a real trust breaker—but he lost the ability to even attempt it on me when I'd left the pack and joined Sun Meadow. Beck had never used his bark on anyone—ever. He claimed he never would. If he hadn't even used it on Arya yet, I was inclined to believe him.

"No one's telling you to," Rory said shaking his head, "I don't know what you're getting so worked up about, all I'm doing is driving us to the complete opposite side of town that Emma and her parents live on. I thought you may want to take the scenic route." Hard pass. "Excuse me for trying to be a hospitable host to you. If I were in your shoes I would want a look at what had changed over the years."

"But you're not me," I said, "And I couldn't care less what changes have or have not taken place in my absence."

Except my eyes were glued to the window like a button sewed onto a shirt. We passed the park where I used to spend hours playing on the swing-set after school making up stories as I flew through the air as a child. We drove past the field where we used to meet with the other teenagers on the week-ends for bonfires and drinks we shouldn't have been drinking.

It was naive that we thought our parents didn't know. They definitely had. In hindsight they played along with it.

Maybe because they didn't care, maybe because they'd rather we got into trouble on pack territory than off of it. If we'd gone into the city to have fun and had a bit too much to drink then the risk of exposure was just that much higher for a teen. Hormones were powerful things, and we were impulsive enough creatures as it was. We didn't need someone shifting in the middle of a human bar because we couldn't get away using fake IDs in the compound.

And then finally, we passed a red brick house with a porch swing whose cushions were a different shade of blue than they'd been when I last swung on it. The hedges had been removed. Rose bushes and other flowers stood in their place. The windows were open, and I imagined there was music playing as the woman who lived there baked something while her husband did something mundane like read the paper or turn on whatever sport was in season. Was any sport even in season in February?

The house was likely decked out in hearts and garland for the holiday. They wouldn't take the Valentine's Day decor down until the first weekend in March. They liked to celebrate love a little longer, they'd say. The decorations reminded them that it shouldn't just be a single day of celebrating your love, but a lifetime of cherishing it.

I guess that commitment only applied to their mates, not their only child.

I wanted to ask Rory if my room had been converted to a craft station or a home gym, but I refrained for two reasons. One, I didn't want him to know I held any interest in my forgotten family. Two, I didn't want to know the answer.

Not really. No good would come of it. Sometimes maybes were kinder than realities.

We were moving slower than we had been—than we needed to be—as we went by the house. I didn't tell Rory to go faster, and he didn't comment on my stare.

This was closure, I thought to myself. I got to see it one last time. This was my goodbye. I'd made my peace with it.

And then she walked out of the front door, and I lost my ability to breathe.

I used to mock people who said their heart stopped beating at certain moments, because how dramatic was that? But as I watched the woman who birthed and raised me lock the door and turn to walk down the porch it felt like mine was surely frozen inside my chest.

Then a pair of honey brown eyes that were a mirror image to mine locked onto me through my window. I wasn't a betting woman, but if I were I'd bet she wasn't breathing either. The keys in her hand dropped to the ground, and Rory brought the truck to a halt.

"Do you want to go out there?" he asked gently, so gently I wondered if he'd mistaken me for a frightened child.

I took my time looking her over where she still stood. Her boots were new but her sweater was familiar. I'd given it to her for her birthday the year before I left. Her black hair had sprinkles of gray, like strands of starlight streaking through the night sky.

"Willow?"

"No," I answered. "Just keep driving."

And as he pulled back onto the road I looked away from

the woman who'd turned her back on me. This time I'd turn mine on her.

"You good?" Rory looked nervously between me and the road.

"Absolutely." I had no choice to be anything else. "I made my peace with this years ago. Why waste more energy than I've already wasted on someone who didn't believe me when it mattered most?"

"Ouch," Rory said, "I guess we deserve that though."

"Yes, you do." He didn't argue with me and I didn't offer further comment. The silence between us stretched on until we were pulling off to the side of the road a hundred or so yards from a house as familiar as my own. From this angle I could see her parents in the backyard gardening and Emma lounging on a chair by the small pond reading a book.

"God she's grown up so much hasn't she?" I asked, more to myself than to Rory, but he answered me anyway.

"There's a big difference between twelve and twenty," he agreed, "even more changes in that time than what changes between twenty and twenty eight."

"Probably," I said, reaching for the door handle.

"It's a miracle she isn't more jaded, honestly." Rory got out of the truck and rounded to my side to open the door before I pulled the handle. I hopped down as he added, "Faye's disappearance was hard on her, on all of them."

I hated that for Emma. I was less sorry for her parents. They were the ones who'd driven her to Miles' clutches in the first place.

"What the hell is he doing there?" The devil himself was

walking out their back door with two glasses in his hand. He strode across the grass until he was towering over Emma who initially shook her head but eventually reached up to take one of the glasses from him. Even from here, I could see her shoulders fall a little further down.

"I told you he looks out for her." Rory said the words as if he expected me to congratulate Miles on his noble efforts or miraculously believe he only had pure intentions.

It simply wasn't happening.

"I really don't like that guy." I whipped my head toward the velvety voice beside me to see Theo glaring at Miles. "That girl's obviously not interested and he's not taking the hint. Is she even an adult? Am I witnessing a crime?"

"She's barely twenty," I told him, "Definitely creepy."

"He isn't creepy," Rory argued, "He thinks of Emma as his little sister. If Faye hadn't disappeared they'd probably be mated by now. He's just trying to take care of the people he thought would be his family."

More like he was looking to start a new one, and mini-Faye fit the bill.

"Did your Alpha take an injury to the head at some point?" Theo asked, looking at Rory in disgust, "He cannot possibly be that naive. A head injury is the only explanation I can think of."

"He's had many, but I don't think they're to blame."

"Pathetic." Theo shook his head in disgust and turned back to stare at the couple I hoped never formed. "I'll be right back."

I didn't watch as Theo carried out whatever nefarious

plan he had in store for my least favorite male, but a spark of joy lit in my chest knowing some sort of retribution would be enacted on my behalf.

"I think it's best we agree to disagree on that for now," I told Rory, "Let's get to what we came here for. Debating Miles' level of creepy is kind of pointless by now, don't you think?"

And I would much rather spend my time tracking down the cloaked figure than trying to explain to a male what he wasn't willing to notice about another. Rory hadn't believed me then, and he wasn't going to believe me now. It was a perfectly timed reminder.

"Where did you see them?" I asked, already walking toward the tree line. He paused, likely debating if he wanted to push the matter further or accept my redirection, before pointing twenty or so yards ahead.

"I saw them there. I tracked them through the trees but lost them at the creek. I'll show you."

Of course they couldn't have used a path. We trekked through the brush of the forest over rocky, twig and root-covered ground toward the creek where I knew he'd lost the scent. I could run a mile in the boots laced over my feet, but the low heel shoes were not made for hiking. A poor choice on my part, but I hadn't been thinking practically when I'd packed.

"This would be better on paws than feet," I grumbled.

"You can always shift," Rory said with a smile, "I'll happily carry your clothes for you. Besides, I'd be lying if I said I didn't miss your wolf."

She certainly hadn't missed him.

"Maybe we'll save that reunion for another day." Like Armageddon. If he tried to pet her he may lose a hand.

"Not thrilled with me, is she?" he asked sheepishly, "I guess that's fair. Mine wasn't overly happy with me during that ordeal either."

I wasn't surprised the wolf had better instincts than the man. I couldn't stop myself from asking, "And what does he think about your dear Miles?"

"My wolf respects the rank I've bestowed upon him." His tone invited no response. We both knew that meant his wolf was likely as weary of the Beta as I was, but pack hierarchy was ingrained in our animals' core.

"This is it."

I took my time walking along the bank, searching for any sign of footprints or evidence left behind that would lead me to their whereabouts.

There was nothing. Not a single indentation in the dirt or snapped twig that appeared in its place, and that alone was enough to make me suspicious. The wildlife was rampant in the woods, and wolves from the pack ran through the space a few times a month. The ground was too perfect to be natural, and maybe that was the key to finding who I was looking for.

I kept walking along the bank toward a row of stones that could be used to cross the rushing water. I just needed to avoid slipping.

I leaped to the first stone and thanked the maker of my boots for at least making the soles grippy in the winter climate. I wouldn't be swept away or drown if I fell into the water—it was far too shallow for that—but I didn't particularly fancy spending the next hour with ice-cold, wet clothes and feet.

"You want some help over there?" Rory called from where he stood with arms crossed next to the water a few yards ahead. "I remember you being a lot of things, Low, but graceful isn't one of them. This may not be your best plan. How about I go grab us some rain boots and we walk across instead?"

"First of all," I said, raising a finger as I wobbled on the small, slippery stone, "How dare you? I have so much grace I'm basically a swan."

His snort was unsurprising but still went ignored.

"Second of all," I raised a second finger, "Maybe you should've thought about that, I don't know, before we drove all the way out here, and I was already on my way across the water?"

At this point I was already committed to crossing, even if the round trip back to get proper footwear would take less than an hour.

"It's your temperature at risk," he said, shaking his head, "Just be careful. If you go down, try to aim for a non-rocky spot."

"I'll do my best," I said dryly.

Because why would I not when the alternative was injury and pain?

"You'll be fine." Theo appeared on the other side of the bank. He leaned against a tree and crossed his ankles while he waited for me. "He's just being dramatic."

"Did you have your fun?" I asked and hopped to the next stone. "I hope someone got it on video."

"Sadly it wasn't caught on camera." He sighed deeply. "I think the message will stick with him for a while though."

I smiled and jumped to the third stone, landing easily. Maybe it wasn't as slippery as I originally worried. The first rock likely just had too much algae or something on it. These were a bit higher, maybe they'd escaped some of the water.

"I hope the evidence is still there when I see him next." If I couldn't avoid the man altogether. "What did you do to him anyway?"

"I simply made sure anyone who looks at him will have fair warning before getting too close using classic means."

I was laughing when I made to move to the next stone. Maybe that was why the moment my toe made contact it skidded up the side of the rock and into the air, tipping me backward in the process.

Three things happened in tandem next. I cursed, Rory yelled my name, and a blast of cold air pushed against me, stopping me from crashing into the water. I hovered in the air a moment, the tips of my hair dipping into the creek. At least the rest of me was dry.

"What the hell?" A rat-like voice yelled from back in the tree line, "She's freaking floating."

"Ugh, why is Miles here?" I groaned while Theo used whatever force it was he used to turn me upright and pull through the air until I stood securely on the bank.

"You could've done that the whole time?" I planted my hand on my hips and looked at him expectantly.

"Yeah, of course." Theo pushed off of the tree and sauntered toward me, flicking the hair out of his eyes as he did.

"Then why didn't you just whoosh me over to begin with?"

"You looked like you were having fun playing hopscotch in the creek." He shrugged. "If you wanted my help I figured you'd ask for it, otherwise I know you have it handled. I only stepped in because I don't think either of us want you to freeze to death. That water is basically liquid ice."

That was sweet. Normally I'd tell him as much, but we apparently had company. I looked to the sky for patience as I prepared to turn and face the Beta who was now on the edge of a full-blown freak out as he demanded to know how I had flown.

"It's been you the whole time, hasn't it?" he accused. "You threw me back yesterday and you put this damn thing on my face, you stupid bitch. What are you, half-witch?"

"You know what, Miles— oh my god!" I had every intention of reading him the riot act but I simply couldn't. I nearly doubled over laughing as I turned to Theo and said, "This is the best thing you've ever done. What did you even use?"

"Fabric dye," he answered proudly, "I found it in the craft room. I know it's usually an A but this felt more appropriate."

"I couldn't agree more." The scarlet C spanned his entire

face from crown to chin and didn't seem like it'd be fading in the near term. It was perfect for the little creeper.

"You think this is funny?" Miles sneered, taking a step toward the water. I dared him to try to cross it. Theo would have all too much fun forcing him into the water—twice, if I was lucky.

"I think it's hysterical," I confirmed, "And no, I'm not half-witch, you moron. You know my entire family, and you've been around me since birth."

Granted, his powers of observation were questionable at best.

"It had to have been you, you—"

"All right, that's enough," Rory's stern tone brought the tiniest of smiles to my face, "Miles lay off her already, will you? She'd been with me the whole time."

"Then how do you explain the shit that's gone down since she got here?" His arms splayed out beside him before falling back to his side in exasperation. "First I land on my back in your driveway like a damn lightning bolt had struck me."

"That's dramatic," Theo quipped, "It was an electrical socket at most."

"Then I have things falling over in my house all night and this eerie whooshing sound ringing out through all hours of the night."

"A classic move," Theo said proudly. I had to agree.

"And now, this," he pointed to his face as the skin around the mark began to resemble the same shade of red as the letter, "appears out of fucking no where, and I come out here to find her levitating on water. What else am I supposed to think, man?"

"I mean it sounds to me like you're haunted," I offered cheerfully. "Anyone you've pissed off or wronged in this lifetime? Any reason something or maybe someone would be popping back into existence at a time like this?"

"What the hell are you implying?" he asked.

"You've been spending an awful lot of time with Emma from what I hear." Rory dipped his head in defeat. Maybe he finally realized I wouldn't be letting this go. "Maybe someone on another plane isn't too happy about it. I mean, what would Faye think of that?"

He charged toward me through the water, soggy shoes be damned, shouting, "You shut your fucking mouth about Faye you murderous little—"

And down into the water he went.

"Can both of you just stop?" Rory yelled, "You're acting like children."

"He totally started it." I claimed with wide eyes and a, hopefully, innocent looking smile.

"I finished it," Theo added proudly.

"Maybe we should just head back," Rory suggested as he lent a hand to Miles to help him out of the stream. If the Beta could shoot bullets from his eyes I'd surely be minced meat by now.

"Fine," I said, "I just want to take a quick look around since I'm already over here. Why don't I meet you at the truck? You can take Hester Prynne there down to get dried off first."

They headed off, Miles cursing me with each shivering step he took while Rory muttered platitudes I'm sure he thought would pacify him.

"What are you looking for, darling?" Theo asked. I scanned the landscape around us, hoping to pick up on the same unnatural state of nature, but I struggled to find it.

"Anything," I answered him, "Anything that's off." Anything that would point me to them.

I continued searching, walking a dozen feet in either direction and making my way a bit into the trees. I turned to go, giving up for the day and hoping something else would pop up in the coming days, but then I saw it.

There, blowing in the slightest of breezes, was a single blonde, corkscrewed strand of hair snagged on a branch. The golden hue sparkled where it waved in the sunlight.

"What is it?" Theo walked toward me from where he'd been searching along the creek. "Did you find something?"

I could tell him everything then and there, I realized. I could explain everything that really happened with Faye, everything I'd been holding in for years, and he'd listen. He'd help. I knew that he would.

If I just opened my mouth and told him the truth, then maybe I could finally share this burden with someone else.

Except, I'd been wrong about who would trust me, believe in me before. What if I was wrong again? What if when I told him everything, he looked at me in disgust or turned his back on me? What if I lost him too?

That wasn't something I was willing to risk.

"No," I lied, and headed back towards the stone path across the stream, "Nothing at all."

CHAPTER 10

Willow

The guilt of lying to Theo left a bitter taste on my tongue, and something told me the too-observant ghost knew it. He'd been watching me more closely since we'd started our descent down the hill to the truck, and hadn't spoken a word since. While I didn't know what thoughts may be running through his head, I felt confident they spelled trouble for me.

We'd been standing beside Rory's truck for a solid five minutes before he walked through Faye's parents' front door followed by her father. A weight settled in my stomach seeing his weathered face.

As a child, our parents always seemed so big, so powerful. Faye's father seemed like one of the strongest, and to see the new lines that had appeared on his face, the touch of white scattered in his hair, was as surprising as it was expected. Eight years of living without his daughter had aged the man I once thought as large as a mountain. And yet, I thought as his eyes narrowed on me, his stare had become no less withering than it was the day I left the pack.

"I need to stay and speak with them for a while," Rory said in a strained voice as he walked toward me, "Miles may have mentioned your visit to the pack to them, and to put it mildly, they have a few questions for me."

"I just bet they do," I said, keeping all emotion from entering my voice, "And let me guess, I'm not invited to join the conversation."

Rory sighed and shook his head. "I'm not sure it would be wise for you to join, but if you want to walk in there with me, I'll support your choice."

"And if they say anything rude to you, there's still some fabric dye leftover," Theo added. "You know I love vengeful arts and crafts. I'm sure at least one of them has dreamt of looking like a clown once in their life."

My lips twitched at the offer. As tempting as it was to see Faye's parents sporting matching red grins, I wasn't interested in listening to whatever insults about me they wanted to share with Rory.

"I'll pass on that reunion, but tell them I said hello, will you?" I requested with a smile. I looked over Rory's shoulder to where Faye's father still stood guard on the porch and waggled my fingers at him.

"I'll be sure to do just that," Rory promised. He reached into the pocket of his jeans and held the keys to his truck out to me. "You can drive back to my house, if you'd like. I don't expect you to wait for me, and I can have someone drop me off when I'm finished here."

I had no desire to sit here and wait for who knew how long while he went inside, but I was also hesitant to take the keys he offered. No one drove Rory's truck but Rory. If I took his keys and drove through town, it would do nothing but draw even more unwanted attention to me. I also didn't want him to think accepting meant more than taking advantage of an escape route.

"We should take it mudding," Theo suggested as he eyed the truck with a mischievous glint in his eye, "I know it's still pretty cold out, but surely the ground has thawed around here somewhere."

"I think not," I told him before turning back to Rory's questioning face. "I don't need the keys. There's somewhere nearby I wouldn't mind visiting."

I nodded my head to the dirt trail peeking out of the woods in the opposite direction. Rory followed the gesture and his eyes softened as he nodded in understanding.

"Fair enough," he said, "It could probably use a visitor or two. I'll come find you when I finish up here."

He gave the now slightly overgrown path one more look before he turned on his heel back toward the house.

I watched him disappear inside, Faye's father following close behind after casting one more nasty look in my direction. I suppose I couldn't blame the man for his displeasure. If I thought someone had killed Faye I'd be a menace toward them as well.

Theo, who didn't seem to share my understanding, made a crude gesture at the man's back that had me giggling.

"I could still go in there," my ghost offered, "No one but

Rory could ever trace it back to you, and something tells me the wolf wouldn't give you away."

He admitted that last part begrudgingly. Rory may very well stay silent on my behalf, but I'm sure I'd still be blamed all the same—evidence be damned.

"They aren't worth the effort," I said as I made my way toward the familiar path, "But I appreciate the sentiment."

I could've sworn I heard him mumble something about choosing another time to make his mark under his breath, but I didn't call him out on it. If Theo wanted to enact a bit of harmless revenge on my behalf, I would simply accept his offering with a smile. For now though, I would rather he stay by my side as we ventured to the next spot down my memory lane.

"So where are we going anyway?" Theo asked as he fell into step beside me. His feet went through each vine and rock I had to avoid with ease.

"A secret hideout," I told him with a smile, "Visitors usually aren't allowed, but I guess I'll make an exception for you just this once."

"I'm touched." He placed a hand over his never-beating heart and said, "I promise to take the secret of its where-abouts to the grave."

My laugh rang through the forest and echoed against the trees. I turned to look at him as I laughed, and my breath caught in my throat.

Theo stared at me with something akin to awe in his eyes. His mouth was set in a soft smile, and if someone had told me I was the only thing in the universe, at that moment I may believe them.

"What?" I asked, still chuckling, "Is there a leaf in my hair or something?"

"No leaves." He shook his head. "I was just thinking."

"About what?" I dared to ask as we followed the curve of the path, the cold-deadened leaves crunched under my feet.

"That if your laugh was the only sound I could hear for the rest of eternity, it would still be a beautiful afterlife."

It took me a second longer than usual to come up with a retort. This felt like something more than our usual back and forth. It was more serious, more real. And *real* was one label I feared giving us, because where could it lead?

"Is that your clever way of saying you prefer me laughing to me speaking?" I asked, forcing a lightness in my voice.

"I'd never say anything of the sort," Theo assured me, reaching over to tuck an escaped lock of hair behind my ear. It was probably for the best, I blushed when the chill of his presence brushed against my skin. I'd likely turn scarlet from the heat of his fingers. "There's nothing I love more than the sound of your voice, whether it's your words or your laughter. Whatever sounds you create, I want them all."

"I'll record myself reading the encyclopedia for Valentine's Day then," I offered teasingly, trying to add some levity back into the conversation. We had one more hill to cross before we reached our destination.

"Does that make me your Valentine?" Theo wagged his brows at me and grinned. I let out a deep breath, thankful for the humor that returned to his tone.

"I mean, as you can see," I said gesturing to the empty forest around us, "The competition for the title is pretty stiff, but if you play your cards right, maybe it could be yours."

"It'd be my life's honor," he assured me, "Would cinnamon rolls and apple crumble help my cause?"

I hummed and tapped a finger against my chin as if considering the notion.

"They certainly wouldn't hurt," I said, "But you may want to throw in a few blueberry muffins for good measure."

He nodded seriously and said, "I'll get right on that for you, darling."

"See that you do." A corner of my mouth drew up in a grin, and my heart warmed at his answering chuckle.

We spent the last few minutes on the path in a comfortable silence, until I looked and smiled at what lay ahead.

"There it is!" I pointed to the wooden structure amongst the treetops, "Our secret hideout."

It was easy to spot in the winter when the leaves had fallen, but it'd been the perfect hideaway during the other seasons. I'd loved disappearing into it for hours at a time as a child, it'd been like escaping to another world. I'd imagined I was a woodland elf hiding in her lair or an outlaw living life on the run.

"Are you sure this thing is stable?" Theo asked skeptically. I tentatively put my weight on one of the boards nailed to the tree trunk, waiting to make sure it was still secure before I began to climb.

"Nope," I answered cheerfully, "But we both know you'll

catch me if I fall, so what's the harm in heading up there to find out?"

"I don't know if I should be concerned for your safety or flattered by your trust in me," he said, floating in the air beside me as I climbed.

"Why not both?" I offered helpfully, "Or neither. I'm going up there either way."

I reached the top of the tree trunk ladder and reached for the latched door above me, being mindful not to lose my grip. As sure as I was Theo would break my fall, I'd still prefer not to risk plummeting thirty feet to the ground below. It took more force than I remembered needing to get the hinges moving, but that was likely the result of years in the elements without use or maintenance.

When the door finally gave way, I carefully pushed myself up through the small opening to climb inside.

It was everything I remembered, yet nothing like I recalled. The paintings we'd added to the walls over the years were visible, but chipped. The string lights we used to lie under were still attached to the makeshift ceiling but half had fallen to the floor. The wires were frayed where they should've connected to the battery pack. Probably the work of a chipmunk or squirrel.

Most of all, everything was dimmer than it seemed before. A fine layer of dust and dirt covered every surface, and the warmth that once entered my chest at just being here was missing.

"So this is where little Willow spent her youth," Theo

mused, looking around with a grin. "You created quite the fortress. Did you do all of this yourself?"

"Not exactly," I admitted wryly, "I mostly supervised and gave the vision. I left most of the execution to Rory and Faye."

Rory had been so proud of himself for getting the little trunks of toys and goodies up the ladder on his own. When we got older he'd been less enthused to be the pack mule, but I always thought he took a secret kind of pride in it.

"When we were kids the three of us would come up here almost every day to play," I explained, walking to one of the trunks in the corner. I choked on a wave of dust that wafted from the lid as I opened it.

"At least these are still here," I said between coughs. The patchwork quilt was just as threadbare as it had been the last time I was here. I was grateful the trunk had preserved it as I wrapped it around my shoulders. The space heater we'd once kept in here was gone, and even if it wasn't, I wouldn't have counted on it working. It was too much of a fire hazard.

Theo drifted around the room, opening and peeking inside every nook and cranny as he went. If it were anyone else, it would feel like an invasion of privacy—a violation of memories that felt too dear to share.

With Theo, it just felt right.

"What's this?" he asked. If not for the cold, I would've surely blushed at the leather bound tome that floated from one of the boxes in the corner.

"That's just an old scrapbook," I said in a tone as casual as

I could manage. My fingers were an inch from snatching it out of the air when it drifted a bit higher then flew into Theo's hands. He couldn't technically touch the pages with his hands, but he moved them as he turned them all the same.

"Just a scrapbook, eh?" he asked from over the top of the book, "Why not look through it together then? Take me down memory lane. I hope there are pictures of you as a kid. I bet you were as adorably vicious then as you are now."

"I am not vicious," I defended, "I'm selectively aggressive. It's completely different."

"Whatever you say, darling," he said in a placating tone before gracefully dropping to hover atop the small bench Rory's father had built us when we were ten. "Sit with me for a while. Who knows when the Alpha will show up to collect you, and call me selfish, but I want to enjoy having you all to myself for a bit longer."

The butterflies that seemed to hibernate in my gut must have mistaken February for Spring because they were fluttering like their very lives depended on it.

"Fine," I relented, taking a seat beside him as I pulled the quilt tighter around me, "But no laughing at me because of anything in this thing."

"I would never laugh at you!" Theo's expression was pure innocence, but shifted the longer I looked at him expectantly. "I don't! I laugh *with* you."

"Sure you do," I muttered and leaned in a little closer to him to peer at the book. The already brisk air was even colder the closer I drew to him, but I didn't move away.

"Is this a scrapbook or a sketchbook?" he asked as he opened to a page with what I thought was a picture of a horse.

"It's a little bit of everything," I admitted with a chuckle when we turned the page and saw a picture of Rory, Faye, and me covered in mud taped to the page. "I liked cataloging everything as a kid whether that meant adding photos or drawing daydreams."

"Yeah?" he asked and turned so his body was angled toward me, "What was it you dreamed about back then?"

"Ponies, apparently," I answered with a chuckle.

"I'll get one for you," he said with a wave of his hand, "but seriously, what did you dream about when you were a kid? Did you always plan to become an Enforcer?"

I hesitated a moment before answering. I hadn't shared this with someone before, though it mattered little. The daydreams of a young child were inconsequential in the grand scheme of things.

"No," I admitted, "I didn't think about becoming an Enforcer until I reached middle school. By then I realized that being the daughter of the Beta pair meant meeting certain expectations—ones I felt happy and privileged to meet."

"Expectations you're happy to meet and dreams you want to pursue aren't the same thing," Theo pointed out. He wasn't wrong.

"Sometimes reality ends up being better than the dream," I countered.

"Sometimes our dreams remind us who we really are

when the world tries to convince us we're whatever it wants us to be." I never ceased to be amazed by Theo's life musings. He was far wiser than one would expect of a ghost who enjoyed writing messages on foggy mirrors and shocking unsuspecting souls for his own amusement.

"I don't think this dream was quite so core to my identity," I offered lightly, "but I appreciate your steadfast support of my past self."

"Past, present, and future," Theo vowed, "I'll support them all. Now stop stalling and tell me. I'm basically re-dying in anticipation."

"Lower your expectations," I instructed with a snort, "It's nothing earth shattering. I wanted to open a tea shop."

"Everything about you is earth shattering," he said almost too flippantly, as if were simply a fact of life, "But a tea shop? I know you love your cozy concoctions, but tell me more."

"My mom and I used to create different blends to test," I reminisced. The memories were somewhat bittersweet now. "We called them our standing Saturday tea parties, and they were the highlight of my week. I wanted everyone to have somewhere they could go and feel as happy as I did then, so why not open a shop for the cause?"

I expected him to laugh or brush past my childhood fantasy, but that isn't what he did.

Instead he asked, "What were you going to call it?"

"I don't think I ever got that far." If I had, I probably wouldn't have chosen a name I'd admit to now. "But I thought it may be nice to put a little bookstore in the shop or a bakery."

"*You* were going to bake something?" he asked in shock. I couldn't blame him. As talented as I was at boiling water for pasta, anything beyond that was a lost cause.

"I may have needed to outsource that piece of the operation," I admitted as another idea dawned on me, "but lucky for me, my future brought me to a ghost who happens to have quite the talent for sweet treats and crafted coffees. Think he'd go into business with me if I asked nicely?"

Theo hummed for a moment as if contemplating a serious business proposal rather than the silly passing thought I'd intended.

"Well," he eventually said, "I'm already set to haunt you the rest of my days. I suppose it wouldn't hurt to go into business with you too, though I doubt they'll accept my name on the paperwork for the loan."

"Fortunately for you, I have an excellent credit score. No cosigner needed."

"Excellent," he nodded in approval. "Then let's discuss decor. I know you love green, but I'm partial to blues, so obviously we'll compromise and the cafe will be green."

I chuckled as he carried on saying, "And I know there's a high demand for coffee in the mornings, but we both know you're grumpier than a gremlin before ten, so we should probably serve high tea in the afternoon. Naturally, I'll handle the menu."

"Naturally," I echoed. "We could even stay open late enough for the drunkards at Howl to walk over and sober up before they head home."

"Sounds like a job for finger sandwiches and macaroni and cheese," he added.

"Macaroni and cheese?" I asked cackling, "At a tea shop?"

"It's our tea shop, darling," he said beaming, "We make the rules and the menu."

Our tea shop. I loved the sound of that. I loved the sound of *our* anything.

"Who would you have recruited to help you if we hadn't met?" he asked, a trace of laughter in his voice. "I can't picture Rory as much of a baker."

"Not at all," I snorted, "He's worse than I am. He'd probably set fire to the oven and burn down the oven on the first day. No, I'd have recruited Faye. She was much better in the kitchen than me, and there wasn't a scheme I could concoct she wouldn't have helped with."

"It sounds like you were quite the pair," he observed sadly, "I'm sorry you lost her."

So was I.

Faye had been the closest thing to a sister I'd ever had before meeting Arya. Losing her had felt like losing a piece of myself, but I had learned to go on without her.

"I'm thankful for the time I had with her," I told him truthfully.

"Coming back here must have raised a lot of those feelings back to the surface," he said slowly, as if waiting for me to contradict it, "I can't imagine what it must've been like to see someone you loved be carried away and be powerless to stop it."

A wave of nausea hit me at the thought, and my brain

struggled to form a response that wouldn't raise his suspicion as to what really happened that day. I settled for a half smile and a hum of acknowledgement instead.

"Are you sure there isn't anything you want to talk about?" he asked despite my silence.

"No," I said with a forced smile, "Nothing at all."

CHAPTER 11

Theo

My little wolf was keeping secrets from me, and I didn't like it. Lying to the Alpha? Sure. No problem. He was pretty much useless when it came to her anyway so I understood keeping things from him, but me? Never.

We didn't keep secrets, at least I didn't think we did until Rory pushed through the doors of Howl, and I watched a steel curtain pass over Willow's face. I'd been trying to pull it back ever since. At first, I thought it was just the man himself. By now I'd surmised the two have never actually dated, but it's obvious to anyone with eyes they eventually would've. That is, if it hadn't been for the whole accusing her of murder and watching as she was excised from her own pack thing.

Then, after I realized she had Rory well in hand—perhaps even a little *too* in hand—I thought it was the trauma of losing her pack and coming back to face her family, but she'd barely flinched passing by her childhood home.

If it were anyone else, I would wonder if it was survivor's guilt knowing her friend was gone while she was still her, but that seemed impossible as well. Nothing about Willow's behavior other than the actual words leaving her mouth made me think she was worried for Emma's safety or heart-broken over her friend.

She'd lied to me earlier. I may not know what she saw in the woods, but whatever it was, it meant something to her. It spooked her. It added another layer to that already solid curtain between us, and I didn't like it one bit. When I asked her again if there was something she wanted to share with me in the tree house, I'd hoped she'd reconsider.

She hadn't.

It hurt she chose not to trust me, but being hurt didn't mean I'd abandon her now. I wasn't quite that fragile. I'd see her through whatever this was whether she wanted me to or not.

Which is what led me here, watching from the trees as my little wolf opened the guest room's window and dropped to the ground without a sound. Her stealthiness was stunning, but it was hard to out sneak a ghost. We could turn invisible and float.

Willow looked around like she expected Rory to pop out from behind a corner or a bush at any moment before she started around the house toward the driveway.

"You little kleptomaniac," I muttered to myself. A smile stretched across my face as I chuckled. I didn't know when

Willow had swiped the keys to Rory's truck, but I watched as she pulled them from her pocket to unlock the door and reach into the cab to do something I couldn't make out.

She was putting it in neutral, I realized a moment later. She moved behind the truck and started pushing it up the driveway. It was good shifters were stronger than witches and humans, or the uphill journey would've been difficult to manage. As well as she was doing at moving forward, the angle was just the slightest bit off with no one to turn the steering wheel.

That, at least, was something I could do to help her. With a flick of my wrist, the steering wheel shifted and her course corrected.

She didn't climb inside until the truck was on the road. The old engine was far from silent. She was wise to wait if she wanted to go unnoticed.

I expected her to head straight for the area we'd surveyed to explore whatever it was she'd seen she hadn't wanted me to know about, but instead she followed a similar route we'd taken earlier in the day.

Ten minutes passed before she got out of the truck and walked to the swing on her parents' front porch.

I could've gotten closer, but it felt wrong to intrude on whatever this moment meant to her. So I kept my distance, and I waited.

I waited while she looked at the front door and took a step closer. I waited while she stepped back and went to take a seat on the porch swing instead. I waited while she rocked the swing slowly back and forth with her heels, and I waited as she rose, reached into her pocket and laid something on the cushioned seat.

When she climbed back into the truck, I stopped waiting. Was it a little invasive to go see what she left on the seat? Yes. Was it less invasive that I waited until she'd walked away? I liked to think so.

Something small glinted in the moonlight. A necklace. The same necklace I knew she kept tucked away in a small box in her sock drawer.

Sometimes I put away her laundry, because she'd been liable to leave it in the dryer for two weeks and use the appliance as a makeshift dresser. When you put someone's laundry away, occasionally you couldn't help but notice things.

Things like tiny jewelry boxes that any sane being would be too curious not to open. I'd expected a ring. I was relieved to find the small necklace instead.

I always wondered if it was an old boyfriend who'd given it to her. I always hoped that the next time I opened the drawer it would've been thrown out or donated—she didn't like to be wasteful. Now I saw it for what it was: a reminder of the home she had been cast out of.

It was the final token she'd been hanging onto for all of these years, and she was finally leaving it behind. I can't say it's what I expected. If anything, I thought her time with the Alpha would be pulling her closer to rejoining that life, not closer to saying a final goodbye to it.

Dread settled in my stomach like a block of lead. She was closing her chapters—saying goodbye, but why? What was she headed toward? What did she expect it to do to her, and why the hell did she think she needed to face it alone instead of just asking me for help? Was it some path for atonement she felt like she needed to take in order to redeem whatever sins she felt marred her past? Screw that.

I'd be by her side whether she wanted me there or not, because where the hell else was I supposed to go? The tail lights of the truck had already faded by the time I pulled my gaze away from the abandoned charm and chain. It didn't matter. I knew where she was heading, and I'd meet her there. Always.

CHAPTER 12

Willow

I didn't slip when I hopped over the stones in the creek this time, which was good because I wouldn't have Theo to catch me if I fell. There was something eerie about leaping over a rushing cascade of black with the glow of the moon as my only light. It was full, because of course it was. Wasn't the moon always full for big moments?

It'd been a full moon the first time I shifted into my wolf. It'd been a full moon the night I realized, or thought I'd realized, that Rory and I were meant to be as we danced in the starlight. It was a full moon the night I left the Thornbridge Pack behind. I guess it was only appropriate it'd be a full moon when I finally faced the cause for it.

I hadn't wanted to exhaust my wolf by running all the way here. You never know what monsters waited in a darkened forest, but as I approached the tree where that single spiraled strand of white blonde had flown, I decided that tonight two legs could only take me so far. That, and my wolf's superior sense of smell, was what had me stripping my clothes and placing them in a neat pile beside the tree. I made a mental note to shake them out before redressing later—if I had the chance. There was no guarantee what I'd find tonight. For what felt like the hundredth time a pressure on my chest drew my thoughts to Theo.

Should I have called for him before embarking? Was doing this alone a mistake? It might have been, but then I pictured the look on Rory's face when I'd pleaded for someone to believe I'd never intentionally hurt Faye—when I begged him to trust me, to help me. It'd felt like a knife on my chest then. I couldn't imagine the pain it would cause to see that expression on Theo's face now.

I sighed as the familiar burn of the change washed over me. Bones cracked, joints popped, and a thick pelt of midnight black fur pushed through my skin until I found myself on four paws, fighting the urge to howl at the glowing moon.

This wasn't a pack run, and this wasn't the time to draw an audience. I pushed off with my back paws until my front landed on the trunk of the tree as I brought my snout closer to the limb to catch the scent.

Cherry and vanilla.

It was faint, but I could work with faint as long as it was there. My wolf followed the phantom of the scent through the woods slowly at first so as not to lose it. The first few miles felt like they took hours for what should've taken minutes.

Then it changed.

The scent grew stronger. My wolf moved faster, sprinting to track the culprit now that I'd passed whatever border had lain around the spell masking their presence.

The stronger it grew, the closer I knew I was to finding them, and it was equal parts joy and anxiety rising from within me as I did.

It had been eight years, eight long years, of thinking this day would never come. That I would never find them.

My legs burned from pushing them to their limits but I didn't slow down. Farther and farther I ran through the trees, dodging bushes and rocks as I went until finally, I ground to a halt. I'd really done it. I wasn't dreaming, I wasn't going to wake up and have this moment ripped away.

There they were.

There, tucked into the hillside was an ivy-covered cottage with a tendril of smoke swirling from its chimney. Golden streaks of warm light escaped from the cracks between the curtain-covered windows.

I could do this, I told myself, I was ready for this. It had to be done. There was no other way to move forward.

Still in my wolf form, I padded over the thick grass of the lawn onto the cobblestone pathway until I reached the front door.

I pawed at the door until the knob twisted and I took a few steps back, leaning on my hind paws ready to pounce if needed.

The door opened slowly, revealing a willowy silhouette with a mane of blue waves atop her head against the light inside.

She didn't see me at first, her eye line too high until a whine escaped my lips and she fixed those violet eyes on me.

"Willow?" she gasped, "Wha—what are you doing here?"

I welcomed the change as it washed over me until I was standing on two feet again. I shivered as the breeze passing through the night air brought pebbles to my skin.

"Hi Faye," I said, crossing my arms over my shivering body, "We need to talk. Are you going to invite me in or should I keep giving the wildlife a free show while you're busy catching flies?"

CHAPTER 13

Willow

Faye jolted like she'd been shocked back into consciousness and stuttered, "Yes, yes of course come inside, God you must be freezing."

She didn't have to say it twice. I was more than willing to comply as she ushered me over the doorstep and into the warmth of the cottage. I mentally thanked whoever was listening that the fireplace was lit as I crossed over to huddle by it, grabbing a blanket from the basket next to one of the arm chairs along the way. I was as comfortable with nudity as any shifter, but it was weird to just lounge around in my own skin even by my kind's standards. Plus, when you see your best friend for the first time in nearly a decade, it felt appropriate to be fully clothed.

"Shit," she shook her head as if to clear it and a wavy lock escaped from her top knot to drape along the side of her face. "I can't believe you're really here, in my living room." Her eyes danced over my blanket-covered form. "And you're still naked."

"Yeah clothes and shifting don't exactly go hand in hand as you know. I had to ditch them by the creek. It was that or carry them in my mouth all the way here, and the little holes my teeth always leave are the worst."

"Don't I know it. Let me grab you something." She darted toward the stairs and jogged up them, calling over her shoulder, "Don't go anywhere!"

"I wasn't planning on it," I mumbled. I didn't sprint through miles upon miles of the forest just to depart after a thirty second hello. I heard her footsteps through the ceiling above me and the slamming of drawers before a door opened and shut.

"These may be a little loose on you." Faye lifted a small bundle of clothing as she descended the stairs, "but they should do the trick. They'll keep you warm at the very least."

I thanked her and grabbed the garments then quickly donned the sweatpants and long sleeve thermal. The pants had a drawstring I could tighten to keep them from falling from my waist, and I pushed the sleeves of the shirt up until they were bunched at my wrists.

Faye had popped into the kitchen while I changed and returned with two steaming mugs, one of which she passed to me. I cupped the heated ceramic between both hands and blew on the still-brewing tea.

"You have a kettle on this late?" I asked in surprise, "I half-expected to be pulling you out of bed at this hour."

"It's the full moon," she said by way of explanation,

"There's too much energy, too much potential, to spend the night sleeping."

I took in every inch of her face as it warred between happiness and trepidation. Time was such a strange thing. In the years that had passed her face had matured in small ways, yet it also felt like she looked exactly the same. We stood there, the crackling of the fire the only sound between us, and stared without speaking. It was as if we both feared that the next word between us could break whatever spell allowed us to be together again, here, in this moment when the rest of our problems lay beyond these walls.

"It is really, really good to see you, Low." Her tone was almost reverent. "But what are you doing here? How did you even find me?"

One eyebrow raised as I asked her, "How do you think I found you?" She had the good grace to look a bit sheepish. "Did you really think whatever spell Nova cast would cover any trace you'd been there? What were you thinking going back?"

"Nova," she said with narrowed eyes, "is extremely powerful so yes, I did think it would cover any sign of me."

"Well it didn't hide every sign of her." I dropped into one of the plush armchairs and curled my legs under me. "I found one of her hairs by the creek and followed her scent here. You're lucky that Rory's sense of smell isn't as strong as mine or he'd have found you weeks ago."

Her usually warm complexion paled as she dropped into the armchair opposite me.

"Rory's looking for me?"

"Technically he's looking for your abductor," I paused then added, "or maybe your murderer, but obviously you've not been kidnapped or murdered so where do you think that trail would've led him? What did you think would happen when you went back there, Faye? That you could repeat the past and no one would get suspicious? What the hell were you thinking?"

"I had to do it," she said, her voice ringing with pure determination, "It was the only way."

As much as I didn't want our reunion to be characterized by anger, I couldn't stop the growl from leaving me as frustration reared its head in my chest alongside my wolf who was ready to throttle her for her carelessness.

"The only way to what? The only way to undo everything we worked for? To throw away everything I sacrificed so you could escape with your little witch in peace?" I looked at the painted portrait of the two of them above the fireplace and chuckled dryly, "What was so important that you had to go back, and don't even get me started on how close to pack territory you built this house. It's like you're asking to get discovered. Is that what you want?"

"Of course not," she snapped, 'Do you really think I would've gone back if there was another way? He's watching her, Willow, I know he is, and I couldn't just sit idly by in the woods while he got his claws into my sister with the rest of the pack practically pushing them down the aisle."

"And making anyone paying attention think she's in danger was going to help?" She had to be smarter than this.

"It worked last time, didn't it?" Faye's chin lifted in the

air. She placed her mug on a crocheted coaster on the wooden end table beside her before crossing her arms over her chest. "If I have to repeat every trick, every trail we made on Emma's behalf I will save her from being mated to a man like him, regardless of if that means I'm discovered after doing it."

"Except it didn't work last time!" I half-shrieked at her. I slammed my own mug down and turned to face her more fully as I said, "No one believed it, Faye, don't you get that? They all thought I murdered you in the woods over that stupid Enforcer position. No one even talked about the trail we'd created or the evidence we planted. Not a single soul in that pack believed you were abducted despite the creepy flowers and cryptic notes. All you're doing is giving him a reason to stick even closer to your sister, all while looking that much more noble and upstanding for it."

Her face was stricken at my explanation. I shouldn't feel angry at her. It wasn't her fault she didn't know what had happened, where this had all led us. I never told a soul what she'd done, and I hadn't asked her where she was going. It had felt safer not to know. All I knew was she was escaping a fate entwined with a male who'd squash her body and soul and that she'd have Nova to help keep her safe.

"I didn't know,"she said softly, "I thought they would believe you. I never considered that they would blame you instead. I noticed you were gone when I went back to check on Emma, but I thought you'd chosen to leave. Willow, I had no idea you'd be driven out."

Neither had I.

"That doesn't matter right now," I said after clearing the emotion threatening to ball in the base of my throat.

"It does," she disagreed in the same soft tone, "If they turned on you, why didn't you just tell them the truth? Even after all this time when you knew I'd be long gone."

"That." The front door opened with a bang and a tall figure entered wearing a scowl so thunderous it rivaled a storm. "Is exactly what I would like to know."

"Rory," Faye gasped and hopped to her feet. Her panicked gaze darted between us, "We can explain."

But I could tell by the set of his jaw, the fire in his eyes that were fixed solely on mine that he wasn't interested in any explanations. He was near a full-blown Alpha rage, and there was little either of us would be able to say before he found a way to calm himself down. Faye seemed to pick up on the fact that it was me not her, at the center of his ire because she rushed over to him, grabbing his forearm as she pleaded, "It's not Willow's fault she was just—"

"Be quiet," he growled. It wasn't an Alpha bark, but it was damn close. He yanked his arm out of her hold and stalked toward me. Slowly, I rose from the chair.

"Eight years?" he asked, "You let me think you'd taken the life of a pack mate for eight years, and you knew she was here, safe and sound the whole time?"

While his tone was accusatory, his eyes looked broken.

"I told you I didn't touch her," I said, "And technically I didn't know she was here, I just knew she was somewhere. I knew that she was safe."

If I knew she'd settled this close to the pack's territory I would've read her the riot act. It was a miracle no one had found them before now.

"Why?" He ran a hand over his mouth and asked, "Why did you do this to the pack, to us?"

"Because the safety of my friends will always be more important than my own standing in the hierarchy," I answered honestly, "It's not my fault you assumed the worst of me instead of trusting me."

"It's because I could tell you were lying!"

The vein on his neck pulsed so strongly I wondered if blood would break through his skin and spray me. That would be a hell of a mess to clean up, and Nova would not be amused when she returned. The witch was a clean freak, though in the case of bodily fluids, I'd have to agree with her stance on cleanliness.

"I couldn't imagine you'd killed her, but I could tell your story was bullshit. I could always tell when you were lying, Low, and you were spewing them through your teeth when you came back from the woods that night."

"I did what I had to do," I answered as honestly as I could, "Faye needed my help, and I gave it to her. I had to protect her."

"From what?" he asked incredulously, "What was it that was worth eight years of all of this? Eight years I'll never get back with you, that her family will never get back with her?"

"From your Beta." He scoffed at my answer and looked away, whether it was to gather his thoughts or say a prayer for patience I didn't know.

"No one needs protection from Miles," he said in a measured voice, "We've been through this before."

And yet he still wasn't getting it. I took a deep breath, preparing to dive into round four hundred and seven of why Miles couldn't be trusted and Rory was too blind to see it when a soft voice broke through the silence.

"I did," Faye all but whispered. Rory and I both watched as she wrapped her arms around herself and stared at her feet where they toed at the floor. "I needed protection from Miles."

"Faye—" Rory began.

"No," she said, her voice growing stronger this time, "I needed protection from Miles, Rory, and you didn't listen. You didn't help me, so Willow did, and you have no right to yell at her for it."

If a feather had fallen to the floor somewhere in the house I think we would've heard it.

Which is why I jumped a solid six inches in the air when a voice over my shoulder said, "Damn, that one's gotta hurt that Alpha pride. I like her style. I see why you were friends with her."

"Damnit, Theo," I said through gritted teeth, "Did you follow Rory here?"

"Don't be ridiculous, darling," he waved the thought away, "I followed you."

"Who the hell is Theo?" Faye asked at the same time Rory demanded to know, "Does he ever just stay home?"

"Not if I can help it," he said cheerfully.

I ignored Rory's question and instead suggested to both

him and Faye, "Maybe we should sit down. I think all of us have a lot to explain, and standing here arguing isn't going to help matters tonight." Or any night. "Let's just shut the door, take a seat, and we'll talk through everything, okay?"

And preferably shut the door Rory had left wide open when he barged in because even if the sun would rise soon, it was still freezing out there.

"Nova's going to lose her mind when she hears—"

"When I hear what?"

CHAPTER 14

Theo

"Hi Nova," Willow greeted the woman in the doorway with a small wave and a smile.

"Willow." Nova lowered the hood of her cloak to reveal a head full of white-blonde curls and bright, aqua blue eyes that danced between us—between *all* of us. "As happy as I am to see you, could someone please explain to me why two wolves and a ghost are in my house?"

"Ghost?!" Faye screeched.

"You can see him?" Willow gasped.

"You can see me?" No one had ever been able to see me other than Willow—no one. So how could this woman? "Can you hear me too?"

Nova untied her cloak from around her neck and hung it next to the embroidered red one on the hooks along the entryway.

"See is a strong word," she said, "but I can definitely sense you. Your voice is faint but it's there."

I wasn't the only person whose jaw dropped open at the revelation.

"I don't know why you all look so flabbergasted," she said as she toed off her boots and walked into the living room to take a seat on the floor next to the fireplace, "I'm a very powerful witch. I sense things. Don't underestimate me just because I live in a cottage and not a castle or the archives."

"Can we back up to there being a ghost here?" Faye looked at the others like she thought they'd lost their senses. "Are we being haunted or something?"

"Theo isn't haunting anybody. He's just my," Willow hesitated before saying, "friend."

Ouch, but what did I expect? We both knew I couldn't be anything more without her sacrificing any hope of a future with a family—which, for the record, I knew she wanted whether she admitted it or not. I saw the look on her face when we passed the family on the street coming into town. It was the same look she had every time she played with one of the pack pups or there was a pregnancy announcement. Longing.

"I don't know," I forced the humor into my voice even though nothing about this felt funny, "I'd haunt you any day."

Nova snorted by the fire, and my grin turned genuine. I forgot how much more fun it was to be my charming self with an audience to appreciate it.

"Okay I can't even see him, and I already know he's adorable," she said.

"Don't feed his ego, I promise you it doesn't need boosting," Willow said seriously, but the upturned corners of her mouth gave away her amusement.

"I think you mean my confidence." I strolled over to the armchair she'd gone back to curling up in and sat on the arm of it beside her. "And we both know you love it."

The pink that tinged her cheeks was a beautiful sight for undead eyes, at least to me. Rory on the other hand was glaring harder and harder by the second. I only *kind of* hoped he gave himself an aneurysm. Despite my dislike for the Alpha for the sole reason he'd once been a contender for Willow's heart, he wasn't the worst kind of man in the world. If nothing else, one look at him and it was obvious to anyone he cared about Willow, even if he'd failed to act on it when it mattered.

"Can we get back to what's important, here?" he asked, crossing the room to lean against the wall opposite from Willow and me beside a painting of a sunset I made a mental note to find out the artist of later. WD loved sunsets and Willow had been trying to pick out a birthday present for her for weeks.

'Who exactly are you?" the Alpha asked the witch.

"I'm the owner of the house you're intruding in," she said with a smile that could cut open a man's soul, "Who the fuck are you?"

On principle, I didn't care for witches. My few encounters with them in life had landed me nowhere but trouble, and I'd taken care to avoid them in the afterlife to avoid further damages. This witch though, this witch I could like.

"I'd rather you two didn't get into a dominance debate,"

Faye said as she took a seat beside the witch and laced their fingers together, "Nova, you already know Rory is the Alpha of the Thornbridge Pack."

"Of Faye and Willow's pack," he corrected, but no one agreed with him.

"And Rory, this is Nova," she said, then looked at the witch with a warm smile as she introduced her as, "my girlfriend."

To Rory's credit, he didn't flinch at the title or look particularly surprised. I would've pegged him for a traditionalist, but maybe there was hope for him yet.

"And she's why you left the pack?" he simply asked.

"Do you ever listen to literally anything we say?" Willow growled, "She didn't leave the pack because of Nova, but congrats to you both, by the way, on the new relationship status."

"Yeah, not so new anymore," Nova corrected, but when you don't see someone for eight years a lot can happen, so it was new to Willow and I thought her congratulations were sweet.

"We'll table that and circle back," my little wolf said then returned her attention to the Alpha in the room, "She left because of Miles. Well, because of Miles and the pack."

Rory's mouth opened a fraction of an inch before locking shut again. He worked the muscles of his jaw as he inhaled a deep breath before releasing it slowly.

"Okay," he said calmly and slid down the wall until he was also sitting on the floor—it was like these people had never heard of chairs before—and looked at Faye when he said, "Tell me everything. I'm listening now."

"Well damn," I muttered, "I was kind of hoping he'd fly off the handle, and I could look down on him for it. I wasn't expecting him to actually stop and listen."

Willow rolled her eyes and Nova's lip twitched, but all of us sobered as Faye dove into her story.

The beginning was almost perfectly aligned with what Willow had already shared with us. Miles had always been a little too interested in her, following her around, warning off the other kids who may be interested in her growing up, or even making jokes about what he'd do to anyone who would try to keep him from her. If you weren't looking closely they were things that may seem harmless, but in the thick of it, if you were the one who feels the hand that's a little too tight on your arm, or you were the one hearing the note that's just a smidge too sharp in someone's tone, it wasn't harmless. It was the first bar in a cage you could see someone building around you but that you still couldn't escape.

The closer they got to graduation, the more intense his attention grew. Miles would show up at her house, acting as if they'd made plans when she knew she hadn't committed to anything. He'd started speaking to her father and hinting that he and Faye planned to start a relationship, planting the seed in her parents' minds when it was the last thing she wanted.

They thought she was just being immature by refusing to admit her interest to her parents. Miles liked to tell them she wanted to make him work for it, that things were better when they were hard to get.

Except a person wasn't a thing. The longer she spoke, the happier I was that I'd all but branded him with the ink. Maybe an actual brand was still called for. I stowed that idea for later. Now wasn't the time.

Later, though, later he would be mine.

When Faye reached the point in her story when she thought that starting her preparation to become an Enforcer would save her from the subtle hints and suggestions from her family about Miles, Rory's skin turned pale. I almost wondered if the little witch or I should summon a bucket in case he was sick.

"All holds were off after that," she said with a shudder, "I wasn't going to be an Enforcer, and having an unranked child was never going to satisfy my parents. It felt like the only thing that mattered to my father after that was to make certain I did whatever it took to ensure I became Miles' mate, and that would've been a living nightmare. Being near him was like having a million bugs crawling on my skin. To actually be *with* him? I can't even imagine."

Neither could I.

I couldn't imagine feeling so uncomfortable and not being able to do anything about it. I couldn't imagine standing there as the people who loved me, who should have protected me, pushed me into something I not only had no interest in but with someone I felt threatened by. The price women pay for boys being boys after society failed to turn them into men was simply too high.

"That's when I got involved," Willow stepped in to explain, "The fight we had was real, but it lasted less than a day. It was obvious to both of us that Miles had found his way into your parents' ears somehow. Things had already gone too far. Asking for help wasn't working so we took matters into our own hands."

Willow went on to explain that they had hoped the topless flowers, the creepy messages—some of which were recycled from Miles' actual notes—and their extended fight were all meant to set the stage to make the abduction story more believable. They did everything they could think of to make it seem like someone was targeting Faye, and someone was, but waiting for him to cross a more distinct line in the sand would have been too long to wait. By then Faye may have been trapped in a forced mating or it could have been the incident that took things too far. She wouldn't have beat him in a challenge then. I suspected my little wolf could tear him apart now.

"You were supposed to get far away and stay gone," Willow chastised with a shake of her head, "What were you thinking settling down this close, let alone your visits to the pack lands?"

"We did!" Faye contradicted, "We didn't come back here until a year ago."

"She wanted to check on Emma," Nova added, "And then she didn't want to go too far in case anything ever happened, so we built the cottage, I set a perimeter enchantment, and now here we are."

"I'm not sure her enchantment was very good if we all made it here," I muttered under my breath."

"Actually it was perfect," Nova corrected with narrowed

eyes, "I only set it up to protect us from anyone who would do us harm."

"Don't you get lonely?" Willow asked, "Why not settle somewhere you can actually go and interact with people?"

"We can do that here," Faye explained, "We just have to wear a glamour."

Too much freaking work if you ask me.

"As interested as I am in your new found social life in the woods," Rory said in a measured voice, "Can we get back to the topic at hand?"

"Right," Faye nodded, "Normally I wouldn't get too close to Emma's house, but I do try to just take a peek every few months, just to see if she's okay, but the last time I was there, Miles was with them at the dinner table with his arm around her chair, and she looked like she'd lost weight."

Faye shrugged.

"I was worried, so I started peeking in more often. I didn't know what to do or how to help," she scoffed, "I wasn't even positive if he was what was causing her to look so haggard or if it was something else, but I did know I needed to stay close."

"I offered to hex him," Nova said simply, "But she turned me down."

"A pity," I said mournfully.

"I went to check in on her on her birthday, still not sure what to do, but then something happened," she paused and looked at the Alpha, "You saw me."

"So it was you in the cloak," he surmised.

"When you chased me I realized that you had to think I

was the same person Willow had claimed abducted me years ago, which gave me an idea." She paused and Nova rolled her eyes before elbowing her in the side.

"Way to ruin the dramatic effect," she grumbled, but continued, "Anyway, it gave me the idea to repeat history. Maybe if someone was worried that Emma was in danger they would pay more attention to what was happening. Maybe someone would notice that Miles is a predator and help her."

"Can we back up for a minute?" Willow asked, "Because what I simply must know is why you thought going back there in that red cloak was a good idea in the first place unless you were trying to be seen from the start. What are you, little red riding hood? Your witch couldn't have altered the color or put a glamour on you?"

I'd been wondering the same. Faye's logic was flawed in more ways than one, but I guess people didn't always think clearly when it came to people they love.

"It's the first thing Nova gifted to me!" she protested, "I couldn't get rid of it."

"And I would've glamoured her if she had bothered to tell me what she was doing," Nova added, "but she didn't. I had to follow her one night to see where she was sneaking off to."

"You would've tried to stop me," Faye said dismissively, "Or said it was too risky."

"It was too risky," the witch said, "And you're right. I would've stopped you, but I also would've helped you come up with a new plan that didn't involve masquerading as a stalker."

"It didn't exactly work the first time around," Willow deadpanned, "No one bought it then, they wouldn't now."

"It made Rory go and find you, didn't it?" Faye tilted her head to one side as if considering, "So it couldn't have been total rubbish."

Rory coming to find Willow was definitely rubbish in my book.

I'd have happily gone the rest of Willow's life and my meaningful existence without encountering the male who was now rubbing a hand across his face as if the simple act could erase everything that had happened. The harsh exhale that left him had all three women turning to watch him. A heavy silence hung in the air as we waited for him to speak.

"Faye," he said, shifting forward so his elbows rested on his bent knees, "I owe you an apology."

I didn't need to hear the sharp intake of breath from Willow to know an Alpha, or really any ranked wolf, apologizing was more rare than catching a star shooting across the sky at sunrise.

"I'm sorry," he said again, "That you were backed into a corner and I didn't help you. I should've listened instead of brushing off your concerns. I promise not to repeat my mistakes."

Rory looked away from a still-stunned Faye to look at Willow, "So you were the mastermind behind the original escape, huh?"

"Someone had to protect her,' she said simply, "If no one else was going to do it, then that someone had to be me."

"And staging an abduction turned murder mystery was your best bet?" He raised a brow, "You couldn't have just had her run away and left a note explaining why?"

A pretty pink scattered across the top of Willow's cheeks as she straightened in her chair.

"Running away would mean if she ever wanted to come back it would be in disgrace. If she was kidnapped then she'd be welcomed with open arms," she defended, then sighed and said, "but maybe there were a few bumps we should've ironed out ahead of time."

"A few?" he asked, "Try a hundred."

"Because your judgement was perfect at twenty?" she scoffed, "Give me a break. I was doing what I thought was best, and I was trying to help a friend. When Miles convinced you and your parents not to make her an Enforcer we knew that taking matters into our own hands was our only choice. His claws were in you too deep for anything else."

"Except he had nothing to do with that decision!"

Rory's anguished growl rattled the cottage, and by the look on Willow's face, her soul.

"What?" she asked, the whispered question was in the exact opposite tone of the Alpha, but was just as cutting.

"Miles had nothing to do with it," he said shaking his head, "it was between me and my parents, and it was temporary. If you had just waited a year—one single year—then an Enforcer position would've opened up, and we had every intention of placing Faye in it once it was available."

"What do you mean it would become available?" Willow asked irritably, "And a year? Anything could've happened in a year, Rory we couldn't wait any longer! She could've been mated by then, and how can you be sure a position would open up? All of the spots were full."

"Because in a year you wouldn't have been in your spot anymore!" he exclaimed, pitching forward, "Your position would've been vacant, and I would've placed Faye in it."

"Oh really?" My wolf scoffed, "And just how was my spot going to magically become available? I would've been a damn good Enforcer, and you know it! No way would I have failed the training or dropped out, so why would it be available?"

"Because an Alpha-Mate can't hold a second rank!"

Faye gasped.

Nova cursed.

Willow's face turned to stone.

And I? I wondered if this was the moment I'd look back on the rest of my existence and realize my little wolf was no longer mine.

CHAPTER 15

Willow

If someone had told me a week ago I'd be standing in Faye and Nova's kitchen washing mugs I would've laughed them off. Yet there I was, scrubbing the same mug I'd been scrubbing for five minutes pretending my entire understanding of the world hadn't been turned on its head in the last two days. Nothing stopped the phrase "Alpha-Mate" from ringing through my mind on repeat like a pop song from the top hits channel.

"I think that one's clean now, darling." The mug was gently pulled from my hands and rinsed under the faucet before floating into the drying rack. I grabbed the next. Theo sighed behind me, but didn't pull this one away.

"Why do you call me darling sometimes?" I'd never dared to ask before, worried that his answer would open Pandora's box or close the door on dreams I knew could never be reality. I wanted to cling to them anyway.

"What, would you rather I called you boo?" he asked, his

usual teasing lilt lacking its usual jolliness. "That seems a bit on the nose given my current status, but I can ignore your lack of sensitivity and roll with it if you'd like me to."

I could leave it at that and move on as if I'd never asked. I could pretend like having him this close to me, speaking just a few inches from my ear, didn't have any effect on me—that *he* didn't have any effect on me.

But he did, and I was tired of pretending.

"Theo." I set down the mug and braced my hands on the edge of the sink. I didn't turn around. "I'm serious."

I looked out the window in front of me while I waited for his answer. The sun was just starting to rise. Streaks of orange and pink had begun to chase away the blackened night sky.

The longer we stood there without his answer, the more tempted I was to give in, to go back to whatever it is we were doing before rather than bring the truth out into the light.

But I didn't. I couldn't give in to the urge to retreat, because where would that leave us? Continuing on our path of building a life together that wasn't *actually* together? Should I keep dismissing every living man I met because he couldn't hold a candle to the dead one haunting my home—haunting my heart—without knowing for sure he felt the same?

No. I needed answers. I needed certainties because with them we could move forward and without them we'd stay in this limbo. My wolf whined at the thought.

We couldn't have it all, but we could have something, I thought as I continued staring at the sunrise, waiting for him to answer me. We may not be able to grow old together, we may not be able to have a family, we may not even be able to hold each other's hand, but wasn't there more to love than those things? Wasn't it going through life with someone, supporting them through the ups and downs unconditionally? Wasn't it simple acts, like doing the chore you hate the most or sitting with you in silence when you're sad? Wasn't love the product of a thousand tiny moments that prove a person puts your wellbeing above themselves?

I saw that life—I was already living it, and if Theo would just say the words out loud, I'd grab it and never let go. If he'd say three little words, we could figure out the rest.

He gave me four instead.

"Rory's a good man." And if my heart had been made of glass instead of stone it would've shattered.

"Right," I breathed the word more than said it. I didn't turn around when I asked, "That's your answer, then?"

"I think," Theo cleared his throat and said slowly, "that he cares about you, and you care about him, at least you did once. You could again if that was what you wanted."

I wanted *you*.

"And what about what you want?" I turned around to face him, the front of my body no more than an inch from the cold plane of what remained of his.

"I want you to be happy," his eyes bore into mine as he said, "and your Alpha is your greatest chance at that."

I waited for him to say something else, to say anything at all that told me he felt a fraction for me of what I felt for him.

But he didn't. He took a step back from me instead. It might as well have been a mile.

"You should go talk to him," Theo said and looked away from me to the doorway that led back to the living room, "I'll take care of the dishes."

If only he'd wanted to take care of me.

CHAPTER 16

Theo

Watching someone you love walk away from you was painful. Watching them walk toward someone who loved them in a way you never could was excruciating.

"That was selfless of you," a lyrical voice commented from the doorway Willow had disappeared through moments before, "Stupid, but selfless."

"It's not nice to eavesdrop, witch." Though it was oddly nice to have someone capable of it again. If we were going to be around someone who could hear me, I'd have to get back in the habit of putting a filter between my brain and my mouth.

Or not.

That sounded like a lot of effort and not nearly as much fun.

"It's not my fault that sound carries in this cottage," she

said wryly, "Though I did build it so maybe it is my fault just a little."

"You did it on purpose, didn't you?" The tilt of her lips was all the confirmation I needed. "So nosey."

"I prefer cautious," she countered and crossed the room to hop up on the kitchen counter, "We were hiding after all. I had faith in my enchantment, but it's always good to be extra cautious. If someone broke into the house I would want to hear it."

I couldn't fault her for that. She'd spent nearly a decade with her guard up in hiding.

"This may be intrusive," I started to ask, "but why are you here?"

"This is my house," she said slowly in the same tone I imagined a teacher would explain the color of the sky to a toddler, "Thus, I am here."

"No." I smiled. The witch was funny. If I didn't have a grudge against all of her kind I would consider making her my second best friend after Beck. "Why did you build the house in the first place? I know why Faye is on the run, but what I don't understand is why you're running with her."

"Ah, that." She nodded her head as she paused as if to consider.

"I was sixteen the first time I met Faye." Her face lit up with a soft smile. "We shouldn't have come across each other, really. My coven and her pack territories were over an hour's drive away, and it's not like shifters and witches are known for mingling."

Understatement of the century.

"I was at one of those under twenty one club nights in the city, and my friends were nowhere to be found. They'd gone off to the dance floor or found someone to occupy them for the night," she waved her hand in the air dismissively, "you know, the usual antics when you're young. I didn't mind. I wanted them to enjoy themselves but it meant I was sitting at the bar alone for a good while."

I knew enough about the girlfriend code from chats between Arya and Willow to know that abandoning your friend alone at a bar—regardless of the presence or absence of alcohol—was a gross violation of it. My wolf—no. Not mine, I reminded myself. The pang in my chest assured me that was bullshit, but I'd mean the words eventually.

Willow would have never left a friend alone in unfamiliar territory. It sounded like Nova's coven was sorely lacking in consideration. It was good she'd upgraded since.

"So you were alone at the bar and they came and sat with you?" I probed.

"Not exactly," she smiled more brightly, "I was sitting at the bar when two males came and sat on either side of me. I tried to give them the hint I wasn't interested, but you know how teenagers can be. They weren't taking the hint."

"That's a character issue, not an age issue," I sneered, "Immaturity isn't an excuse for making unwanted advances." And I didn't know why she was smiling like that was a fond memory. I was irritated just imagining it.

"Right you are," she agreed, "But not the point of this story. One of them grabbed my arm, and the other kept crowding closer to me. It felt like I was suffocating."

Disgusting excuse for males.

"And that's when I saw her." Nova sighed and kicked her sock clad feet against the cabinets below her.

"Faye?"

"No," she shook her head and said, "Willow. She ripped the men away from me and gave them a dressing down that caught the attention of half the club even with the music blaring."

Warmth flooded my chest. Even as a teenager she'd been so strong.

"The bouncers eventually came over to help escort the men from the club, and Willow had a word or two for them about the safety of the club's patrons for them as well."

I didn't doubt it for a moment.

"She asked me why I was alone and looked appalled that my friends had abandoned me. She declared right there and then that I'd join the Thornbridge Pack table. She promised they'd look after me the rest of the evening, and that's exactly what they did."

She blushed when she said, "Faye was one of the other shifters at the table and pulled up a chair for me. We talked through the night, exchanged phone numbers and the rest was history."

Puppy love—literally. How cute.

"So you fell in love," I observed, "And you left your coven behind for her?"

"It wasn't instant love," Nova corrected, "At first it was just a friendship—the very best kind of friendship. It's a longer story for another time, but a year later I was excommunicated from my coven for refusing to participate in a ritual."

Refusing the coven leaders was definitely grounds for expulsion, but a full excommunication? That was nearly unheard of. Nova seemed less than willing to delve into the details of her banishment, and I suspected the 'another time' she referenced would be the day hell froze over.

"That must have been very hard," I said in what I hoped was a comforting tone.

"I managed." She sat up a bit straighter on the counter. "The point is when Faye became pack-less, I had already lost all ties to my community. Helping her disappear when she and Willow asked me for help was simple, and the decision to go with her was even easier. The love between us came later."

"Well, I'm glad you get to be with the person you love." I certainly couldn't. It was a luxury people too often took for granted.

"I wouldn't be without Willow." Nova's voice dropped to a low tone, and she lifted a hand to beckon me closer. I went. "Is pushing her back into Rory's arms really what you want? Do you really think he's what's best for her?"

Of course not.

"I think she deserves a life of love and happiness." My answer was evasive but honest. She deserved to have everything she wanted in life, and if the Alpha is who could give it to her, then I'd accept a lifetime of longing for her to have it.

"I'm sure you do," Nova mused. She tilted her head toward one shoulder, then the other.

"I do."

Her eyes narrowed as she studied the area around me before they went wide.

"You're not what you seem, are you?" My heart beat faster in my chest, though there was no blood to pump through my veins I swore I could feel it pounding. "You aren't really dead."

"But I'm not living," I clarified, "Not really."

"A nasty curse," she said with an upturned lip.

"Witches can be nasty creatures." I was pleasantly surprised by the one in front of me, but it didn't change my view on the rest.

"You know, Willow has done so much for me," she drawled as a cat-like grin stretched across her face, "It'd be my honor to do something for her in return, and like I said, I am a very powerful witch."

"What do you—" I never finished the question. Nova's hand shot out to rest—actually rest—on my forehead and then there were no words left to utter.

There was only light.

CHAPTER 17

Willow

He didn't want me, at least it was that or he didn't want me enough. Maybe it had all been in my head, I questioned as I trudged over the wood flooring of the hall toward the living room. I'd passed Nova on my way out of the kitchen, but I assumed I'd find the others still there. A trickle of warmth ran across my cheek, and my fingers were wet when I swiped it away.

I did not cry when I'd said goodbye to Faye.

I did not cry when my pack had thought the worst of me.

I did not cry when Rory had turned his back on me.

I refused to cry now over a love that was never truly mine.

Faye was sitting in the armchair I'd been in earlier when I walked back into the room. Her gaze met mine as she inclined her head to where Rory stood across the room. I glared at her waggling eyebrows and subtle smirk. The words 'I told you so' were unspoken but understood after years of this childhood debate. She'd said a hundred times that Rory would ask me to be his mate one day, and as much as I'd hoped it to be true at the time, I'd brushed off her predictions each time she said them aloud. Logically, I'd known that I was the most suitable match, but suitability and true sentiment didn't always go hand in hand.

Faye moved her head in a motion so violent I half wondered if it would detach from her neck. My hands came up in surrender and I started toward Rory.

If I hadn't felt like my heart had been ripped from my chest a minute prior, I'd probably have noticed the way the warm glow of the fire highlighted the angular lines of his face. He leaned against the fireplace with a forearm across the mantle and stared into the rolling flames as I approached.

"So," I said intelligently from where I stopped at his side, "Eventful few days, huh?"

I knew the humor I tried to inject into my voice fell flat, but I wasn't sure how to break the tension that had grown between us since he revealed his plans from years ago.

One corner of his mouth drew up as he said, "You could say that."

The problem was, I wasn't sure what else I could say. Should I say I was sorry that I hadn't read his mind when we were teenagers? Should I ask him why he never cued me into his plans instead of acting on his own? That answer was obvious, he was a born Alpha. He rarely, if ever, stopped to consider reading someone in on his plans before he deemed it necessary. And what would be the point of me digging into the past, anyway?

Whatever window that had been opened without my

knowledge had surely closed by now. We weren't the same people. We didn't want the same things. We weren't even in the same pack. The future that could've existed for us had long disappeared.

Except what if it hadn't?

"I wish you would've come to me back then," he said finally, "I wish I had made you trust me enough to come to me instead of feeling like you had to solve this alone."

I'd tried, is what I wanted to say, but why rub salt in an already raw wound?

"I wish we'd been able to speak openly," I said instead. It was the truth, and yet if we had I wouldn't be where I was today. I wouldn't have met Arya and Beck, I wouldn't have settled into the Sun Meadow Pack, and I would've never met Theo. Though if I hadn't met Theo, maybe I'd be feeling better right about now. Maybe I still could. After all, hadn't Theo all but told me to go after Rory? Communication didn't get much clearer than that.

"We've lost a lot of time," he said sadly, shaking his head slowly. The glint of the fire light twinkled in his eyes as he moved. He looked up and gestured to Faye who was still curled in the chair, pointedly pretending she wasn't eavesdropping. "We all have."

"Well it's a new day," I said and forced a smile as I looked out the window toward dawn's light creeping in, "Where do we all go from here?"

A slew of emotions from frustration to sadness to resolve washed across his face as he considered.

"I don't have the right to tell Faye she should return to

the pack or see her family," he stated, "but I do have the obligation to make it safe for her to feel like she could do those things if she wanted to. When I go back, Miles and I will be having a long conversation about what is and isn't becoming of a Beta—or any male—in this pack. I'll also talk to Emma and give her the chance to explain anything she wants to share, but I won't make her."

From the corner of my eye I watched as Faye quickly reached up to wipe at her face, and I swore I heard a sniffle. If the tears were from relief or years of heartbreak coming out, I couldn't say, but I hoped it was the former. She deserved to have a safe home to return to if that was what she wished, but I couldn't imagine the difficulty she would face if she ever spoke to her parents again. In her shoes, I wouldn't know how to forgive them for pushing me to my limits. I didn't even know how to forgive mine, and they hadn't believed the person causing me the most harm over me. They just hadn't believed in me to begin with.

"That's good," I said softly. Despite my wolf's protesting growl, I reached up and laid a hand on Rory's shoulder. It was as hard as a rock. I gave it a quick squeeze hoping to ease some of the tension plaguing him. "We can't go back and change the past, but we can figure out how to move forward."

He turned his head from the fire to me and asked, "Can we?"

"Yes, of course, you just said—"

"Not all of us," he corrected, his eyes darting between

mine like they were searching for some buried secret in them, "You and me. Can we find a way to move forward?"

There are few moments in life where I believe the phrase *time stood still* was appropriate, but this was surely one of them.

I could pretend not to understand—and hell, maybe I didn't. I could acknowledge that we'd moved past our previous hurts, or at the very least resolved them, and suggest we part on good terms.

Then, there was the third option.

I could say yes and see what this future could look like if I gave it a chance. Rory had made mistakes, but he was trying to learn from them. He was gentle and kind, but still a strong leader for the pack to lean on. He believed the best in people, sometimes to a fault, and he used to know me better than I knew myself. Until he didn't, I suppose. But more than anything, just like Theo had said, Rory was a good man.

"Maybe." It was the best answer I could give. I should've left it at that, but the next words that left my mouth slipped out before I could censor them, "Why didn't you tell me?"

"Low," he started, but I held up a hand to silence him.

"Why didn't you tell me what you wanted us to do, to become?" My voice broke on the last word when I thought back to the anguish I'd felt as a teenager falling in love with the boy who I thought would never love me back. "You were making a decision that affected both of us, so why couldn't you have just told me?"

Rory pushed off the mantle and stepped closer to me, one hand reaching up to cup my jaw, the tips of his fingers threading into my hair. He smiled wryly and asked, "Because your judgment was perfect at twenty?"

A small laugh escaped my lips at having my own defense throw back at me. I would've applauded him for it, but that was the moment that Nova walked into the room and clapped her hands together.

"Ta-da!" she said and splayed her arms out to the side to reveal a sight that had my still-gripped jaw dropping.

"You're welcome," she added cheerfully and dropped onto Faye's lap, wrapping an arm around her girlfriend's shoulders. I could barely hear her murmur, "Baby, we should've made popcorn because things around here are about to be better than a holiday rom com."

"Because they were so dull and boring before," Faye grumbled back. She continued speaking, but the words were lost to me as my eyes locked with a pair of sky blue ones standing in the doorway.

"That isn't possible," I gasped, stumbling back a step. Rory's hand fell from my face and his solid arm wound around my back to steady me.

"Who the hell are you?" he asked the man with swooping blonde hair, and a dimple that appeared as one corner of his mouth rose. He didn't spare Rory a glance, staring straight at me even as he answered.

"I'm Theo."

CHAPTER 18

Willow

We hadn't ended up flying home like we thought we would. It turns out when your traveling companion is a man who until recently had been a ghost, you still needed legal identification to get on a plane. The packs had connections, and they were good, but not that good. It would take at least two days to get the necessary documents created, but after seeing the look on Miles' face when Rory relieved him of his position as Beta, I had no desire to stick around and wait for them. Not to mention, staying longer meant risking a run in with my parents and some bridges were best left burned.

Rory had offered to drive us back, but being trapped in a car with *both* of them was a 'no way in hell' scenario for me. Which is how I found myself in a too-small rental car on an eight hour road trip with the man who'd all but rejected me less than a day prior.

"We're about twenty minutes out," I murmured to Theo

who was reclining in the passenger seat. I was beyond ready to be out of this car to have some distance between us. The close proximity had my wolf near jumping through my skin to touch him, and I simply couldn't have that. I knew she was a fan of the man before he was, well, a man again, but she could at least try to have some self-respect. I wouldn't be shocked if she begged him for a belly rub on my next shift.

If he was still here for it. I hadn't voiced the question plaguing my mind, but refusing to ask it didn't make it go away. There was nothing tying him to this place anymore.

Everyone could see him.

Everyone could hear him.

So why would he stay with me now that he could be with anyone else?

"I can't wait to see Skye," he said with a bright smile, "I bet her fur is every bit as soft as I imagined it."

Well, maybe he would stay for the dog.

"We use the good shampoo," I noted, "Her fur is perfect. Don't be hurt if she doesn't recognize you at first though, it's not like she'll know you were the magical force scooping out her meals every day."

"She'll know," he said with certainty, "and if she doesn't I'll win her over quickly enough."

"Oh yeah?" I asked, grateful to be having a conversation that felt halfway normal with him, "And how do you expect to manage that?"

"Dog treats and snuggles." The *obviously* was implied but remained unspoken. "Plus I have my extremely lovable disposition. She'll fall for me eventually."

Didn't we all?

"If you say so."

The silence we fell back into was more comfortable than it had been before. I didn't think we'd spent more than a handful of minutes without one of us, usually Theo, speaking or commenting on what we were doing in years. Sitting next to one another and exchanging nothing but stilted small talk for hours on end had felt wrong on every level of my being, yet I didn't know what else to do.

"Willow," he said in a more serious tone than I would've liked, "About the other night—"

"Oh, look!" I said far too brightly and much too loudly for the confines of the car, "We're here!"

Thank God for small miracles like men waiting to have difficult conversations until the end of a journey. If he'd mustered the nerve, or maybe simply considered saying whatever it was he wanted to say earlier in the trip, there'd have been no escaping it.

Then, again, that was so Theo, wasn't it? He'd never back me into a corner I couldn't duck out of. He was simply too damn considerate to think of it—at least he was to me. I suspected others may receive less of his thoughtfulness, but they hadn't been the ones to keep him company while he walked the earth all alone. Maybe now someone else would be.

"Willow, I really think we should—"

"Arya's already here!" I interrupted again.

I'd never been so happy to see my best friend in my life. I wasn't overly surprised to see her sitting on the porch swing with Skye at her side. What looked like an ACE bandage was sticking out from her sock—courtesy of Theo's creative messaging system. I'd given her our ETA and there was a little doubt in my mind she'd patiently wait for a recap of the past few days. I was, however, surprised to see the man she was arguing with.

"And so is Beckett," I also noted.

"WD probably did something like walk here on that ankle alone to piss him off," Theo guessed.

I put the car in park and asked as we unbuckled our seatbelts, "Please don't call her that to her face. I will literally never hear the end of it."

He shrugged with an impish grin. "No promises."

Theo was ducking out of the car and closing the door behind him a split second later. Instead of heading toward the porch to wreak havoc with a healthy dose of heckling as I expected, he rounded the front of the car until he was at my door, hand on the handle. When it opened, I'd like to say I slid out gracefully and rose to stand beside him. In reality, I sat there in shock for a solid four seconds before attempting to get out of the seat. Unfortunately, my still buckled belt made that rather difficult.

"Careful there, darling. Let me help you with that."

He smiled and I held my breath as he leaned into the cab of the car toward the buckle. His chest had no business being so toned in his black thermal shirt when he hadn't even had muscle mass twenty four hours prior. What was even more distracting was the heat coming from his body. I'd developed a fondness for the chill his presence brought to the air, but the heat emanating from him was something else entirely. Between that and his scent, my wolf was practically purring like a cat inside me.

Theo's scent was the kind of smell that wrapped you in a cozy blanket on a winter day, but had a hint of danger to it. Bourbon, orange, a hint of vanilla—he was the male equivalent of an old fashioned, and damnit if I didn't want to curl up by the fire and sip from that glass all night lo—no! *No sipping*, I chastised myself and my wolf. Her responding whine bordered on pitiful.

"There you go." I swore he moved slower than he needed to stand back upright. "Shall we?"

This time when I went to exit the car, nothing hindered me but my own shaky legs. It was just from sitting so long on the drive, I told myself, it certainly had nothing to do with the man lingering a few inches away.

"Bitch, you better get up here and explain yourself," Arya called from her spot on the swing. The man on the moon could likely see her smile from space.

She went so far as to waggle her eyebrows as we walked toward the porch. Skye, who had been lying peacefully beside her perked upright. She jumped from the swing, knocking it and Arya off balance, and bounded towards us. She bypassed me and dove straight into Theo's arms. He sent me a smug grin over the top of her head as a clear 'I told you so.'

The traitor.

"Well hello there, handsome," Arya called. She pushed a scowling Beck away from where he'd gone to steady the porch swing, and headed in our direction, "I can't say you're the male I expected to see get out of Willow's car, but I'll withhold any complaints. For now, at least."

Beckett's growl only had her grin widening as she moved across the steps. If I wasn't mistaken, she had a slight sway in her hips that wasn't usually there. Whether it was for Theo's benefit or Beck's I really couldn't say. The effect was decidedly ruined when her toe caught on a plank I'd been meaning to fix.

Arya cursed as she pitched forward down the porch steps. Beck, caught her before her face could make contact with the dirt, but as soon as she was stable, he dropped his hands from her waist like the contact burned. All he earned for his efforts was a huff and a glare as she continued by him.

Early on in our friendship I'd tried to ask her about whatever it was between her and our Alpha, but she'd shut it down every time—hard. I'd let it be since, but there were moments like now, moments when I watched the way Beck's face softened for just a moment when he looked at her, that biting my tongue felt ten times harder.

"Damn, WD," Theo said with a chuckle, "No need to literally fall all over me. We've only been apart for a few days."

I glared at the nickname, and he shrugged.

"WD?" Arya asked, perplexed.

"Willow, who is this guy and what the hell was he doing with you two a few days ago?" Beck's question wasn't a bark, but there was no humor in his voice. Unfortunately, his lack of humor didn't tamper Theo's in the slightest.

"It's really hurtful you don't recognize me, Beck," he said with a mock pout and placed a hand over his heart, "And to think I considered you my best friend. It's like our years together have meant nothing to you."

Arya looked at Beck wide-eyed. The Alpha looked borderline horrified at Theo's antics, and a giggle escaped my lips.

"Beck, Arya," I informed them, "This is Theo."

"What the—"

"The ghost?"

"About that." I sighed and ran a hand through my hair before raising it toward the front door. "You should probably come inside. I have a lot to catch you up on."

BECK AND ARYA HAD BEEN MORE THAN A LITTLE intrigued by our account of the past few days with the Thornbridge Pack. He was even less keen on having a warlock—because of course Theo, the apparent *warlock*, kept his magic from beyond the grave—living in his pack's territory. I'd been more than a little surprised when Theo whisked our bags into the house from the trunk of the rental car with a swish of his wrist. Or rather, he'd whisked my bags into the house.

Another problem with returning from the dead was not actually *having* bags, or any belongings of his own at all. As cranky as Beck was about this newfound situation, he'd kindly run home to grab a few of his own things for Theo to borrow until we could head to the store. He'd also brought an air mattress which would be much more comfortable for Theo to sleep on than my couch.

We'd left the Thornbridge Pack at the crack of dawn that morning, and the exhaustion must have shown on my face because Arya had let Beck drive her home with minimal protest once things were settled.

I knew it would only be a brief reprieve even before she called over her shoulder, "Don't think you're off the hook Willow! I'm giving you today to recharge your emotional batteries and then your ass is mine!"

"Whatever you say, Ari," I said back as Beck herded her into the passenger seat of his SUV.

"I mean it!" she yelled out the window, "I'm talking a full on sleepover and if you skimp on one detail or one question, I'll know!"

"Keep your head in the car, Arya!" Beck growled. Their bickering rang through the air as they pulled away.

I'd chuckled as I turned to walk back in the house, only partially surprised to see Theo leaning against the open doorway grinning back at me the way he had a million times before. Except this wasn't the same as it was before. Nothing could be, and I didn't have the slightest clue where we'd go from here.

"Do you think Beck will make me his best man at their mating ceremony?" Theo asked as we entered the living room. He crossed the room and dropped onto the couch where Skye quickly curled up at his side. He absentmindedly stroked her fur as he awaited my answer. Lucky girl.

"I'm sure you'll find a way to convince him to, even if he

doesn't." Even if it meant pulling a surprise appearance at the altar. "You have a lot of time to plant the seed. I doubt those two will get over their issues any time soon."

"They may surprise you," he countered. "Things sometimes have a way of working out a lot faster than you may think."

If only we were the couple he was referring to instead of Arya and Beck. Or maybe he wasn't referring to any of us. He had, after all, just been given a new chance at life—a chance I was sure he hadn't planned to ever receive.

"Did your recent resurrection turn you into an optimist?" I asked, still standing. I could take a seat in the armchair, but he knew I considered it the most uncomfortable thing on earth. I'd purchased it solely because I liked the mustard yellow color and cozy aesthetic. Only unwanted guests were encouraged to sit there.

But if I didn't sit in the chair, the only other spot for me to slide into was the space between Theo and the armrest of the couch. Skye had splayed out to occupy the other cushions.

"I'm not an optimist," he said, answering the question I'd already forgotten I asked, "I guess I just like the idea of being with you when you walk down an aisle."

"Excuse me?" Surely he had not just said what I thought he'd said. Especially after drawing what felt like a clear line between us in Faye's kitchen.

"I mean, you'll be Arya's maid of honor, right?" the tilt to his lips told me he already knew that isn't where my thoughts had gone. "Or does she have another best friend or sister I've never heard of who'd claim the role?"

"Of course I would be." At least I better be. I wouldn't consider myself particularly possessive, but I had once licked Arya's hand when she tried to cover my mouth. As we all knew, that meant she was mine. I didn't make the rules. I licked her. She was mine.

"Then like I said, I'll be with you when you go down the aisle," he said as he leaned back into the couch. "You know, when Beck makes me his best man."

"Right," I drew out the word, finding, yet again, that I wasn't sure what to say. Speaking with Theo when he was literally out of reach had been almost effortless. Now I felt like my tongue was tied in knots every time he turned that boyish grin I'd always loved so much my way.

"Are you going to sit down?" he asked, nodding his head toward the empty spot beside him, "or do you have a newfound love for standing in the middle of the living room all night? You can if you want to, but I'd recommend sitting. I think we have a lot to talk about, don't you?"

We did, and it was far too much to tackle sitting that close to him. I'd rather stay in this limbo we'd found ourselves in than hear him tell me to go pursue a life with another man again.

"Can we just not, tonight?" I asked. "I don't think I can handle another emotionally charged conversation this week on top of everything else that's happened."

"Who said anything about it being emotionally charged?" he asked, raising one golden brow.

"Anything that requires me to think is considered emotionally charged right now," I argued, "I just want to go upstairs, take a shower, then come down here and exist for a bit. Can we do that?"

He didn't agree right away, and I feared he'd push the subject and insist we talk through whatever it was our future held tonight.

"Please, Theo? Can we just give this new reality a day or two to set in?" I pleaded softly.

"Okay, darling," Theo agreed, nodding his head. "We'll give ourselves a couple days to figure out our new normal."

"Thank you," I breathed a sigh of relief.

"Thank you for telling me what you need," he said then suggested, "Why don't you go upstairs and take that shower. You'll feel better after you stand under the hot water for a while. Then you can come down here and we'll watch that movie with the hand flex you like so much. Okay?"

An emotion I wasn't quite ready to name welled in my throat as I whispered back, "Okay."

CHAPTER 19

Theo

Willow was freaking out the hell out, and there was very little I could have done to stop her. In all fairness, she'd revisited the pack that all but cast her out, reunited with her presumably dead best friend, spent days working beside her first love, and had the ghost haunting her house get resurrected in a matter of days.

A little freaking out was warranted.

If taking a few days to adjust to our new normal was what she needed to calm whatever panicked voices were sounding in her head, I could give that to her. Sadly for me, giving her the time to process before we addressed the elephant in the room was near torturous.

I longed to take back everything I'd said to her in Faye and Nova's kitchen. I wanted to tell her that Rory may be a good man, but he would never be her man. That role was reserved for me, and after all of these years together, surely we both knew it. I wanted to wrap my arms around her. I wanted to tell her I loved her—and I would. In a few days.

If she needed time, I would give it to her, because no matter what it was I wanted, her needs would always come first. We didn't need to rush, and a life with her would always be worth the wait. I just hoped that's what she wanted.

She and the Thornbridge Alpha had looked more cozy than was comfortable by the fire last night, and had embraced a second too long before we departed at the crack of dawn this morning. He'd whispered something in her ear too low for me to hear. Whatever it was, she'd smiled up at him like he'd held all of life's answers and offered to share them with her. I didn't like it; I only wanted her to look that way at me. I may not have all of life's answers to offer, but I'd look for them alongside her if she let me.

But before I could tell her that and more, we had a movie to watch.

While Willow disappeared into the master bath, I'd taken advantage of the guest bathroom down the hall. There were few things that felt as good as standing under the scalding water after a decade of feeling nothing at all. I probably stayed in there too long, because when I stepped back into the hall, rubbing a towel against my still-damp hair to dry it, Willow was already on the couch in the living room.

I didn't even pretend not to enjoy the way her eyes seemed to take in every inch of me, her mouth parting ever so slightly the longer she stared. I hadn't seen her stare at Rory once that way.

"I'll happily stand here for you all day, darling," I said with a wink, "but should we at least put the movie on so you can pretend to stare at the screen instead?"

The pink that rushed over her cheeks was a beautiful sight. She gave her head a shake before stammering out a response.

"So-Sorry," she said, "I guess I'm just not used to seeing you when I can't see through you. The whole solid body thing may take some getting used to."

Well, she could explore my solid body as much as she'd like as long as she kept looking at it like that. She could stare at it, touch it—hell, lick it if she wanted to and I'd happily let her. But sadly for me, that would have to wait along with our chat.

"All good," I assured her, "It's a pretty big change for both of us."

I tossed the towel to the side and waved a hand to send it back to the bathroom towel rack to dry. I could've sworn she mumbled something along the lines of "he even cleans up after himself," and I fought the urge to laugh. If hanging up a wet towel instead of tossing it somewhere in a heap was the standard, my gender really needed to work on raising it.

I sat on the couch beside her, probably closer than she expected, but still leaving a few inches between us. I reached for the remote and asked, "Shall we?"

She nodded and grinned, but didn't seem to relax as I hit play and the now too familiar instrumental music came through the speakers. I'd seen this movie no less than fifty times with her since she'd moved in to the previously vacant house I liked to haunt.

I draped my arm along the back of the couch behind her. It took a few minutes, but eventually she leaned back and started to relax. I loved the way she murmured her favorite lines in sync with the actors on the screen and chuckled at the same jokes she already knew were coming.

Every shift in weight or minor move as we watched seemed to draw us closer together until her side was nearly plastered against mine as we watched. It was so tempting to move my arm from the couch to curl around her shoulders, but if I did, she may pull away entirely. I wasn't ready to break whatever this bubble we'd found ourselves in was, so I held perfectly still and enjoyed each accidental graze of her arm or brush of her hair.

By the time the credits were rolling across the screen, the sun had gone down and the only light in the room was the glow of the mostly black screen.

"Gosh, I love that movie," Willow sighed as she dropped her head back against the couch—and my arm—to look up at me. "I think I could watch it every day and never get tired of it."

"Whatever makes you happy, Willow," I said offhandedly, daring to raise my hand from its resting place to run along the soft waves of her onyx hair. She stiffened beside me, and some of the care-free joy that had finally appeared left her eyes.

"Right," she said and leaned forward, her elbows coming

to rest on her knees, "Because that's what you want, right? For me to be happy?"

She pushed up from the couch to stand, and it became more than obvious by the set of her jaw and closed expression on her face I'd made a misstep.

"Willow—"

"Are you hungry?" she asked. "I'm hungry. We should pick something up for dinner. I doubt either of us are in the mood to cook."

"I mean, yeah." I stood from the couch and hurried to throw on my shoes while she grabbed her car keys. "I could eat, but Willow, why do I feel like we just had an entire conversation I just missed? Did I say something wrong?"

Had I made her uncomfortable? Was the hair touching too much? Was I wrong about us being on the same page about what this was—what we could be? Had she made promises to Rory and I crossed a boundary I didn't know existed?

Willow's entire body seemed to sag as she exhaled and said, "No. Of course not. I'm sorry, I'm just tired. I probably waited too long to eat, and you know I get cranky when I'm hungry."

Her laugh fell flat, but I didn't call her on it. She'd asked me for a few days of semi-normal. It was my fault for pushing.

"Then let's go get something to eat," I said before reaching around her to open the door. "After you."

"Thank you," she said. Whether she was thanking me for opening the door for her or not pushing her to explain her sudden shift in mood, I couldn't say. "Let's just go to Howl. If they're too busy we can get it to go and eat here instead."

"Perfect." I smiled as we crossed the driveway to climb into her car. "Beck probably misses me by now."

The weight on my chest lessened, because this time, the laugh that left her was anything but forced.

CHAPTER 20

Willow

"Seven years of friendship, and you never thought to mention the ghost haunting your house was hotter than a fried egg on a summer sidewalk?"

"That is not an analogy people use," I pointed out because honestly, how could I not?

I dodged the pillow she threw at my head as she growled, "Don't change the subject! We have important matters to discuss, damnit."

We were on my bed, in pajamas—mine, and they were more than a little too loose on her, but at least they weren't too tight, no one wants tight pajamas—drinking tea that Theo had brewed for us.

Because apparently the man's acts of service weren't limited to his time as a ghost, and he could, in fact, work a kettle using his corporeal hands. Arya had taken her mug from him and looked at it like a pot of gold. It was the same look Paisley had given him when he kept her from slipping on a stray splash of water at Howl the night before. I finally understood Arya's frustration with the sunny waitress when I watched her beam at Theo while she waited on us the rest of our meal.

I made a mental note to tell Beck he should try bringing Arya tea next time they were at each other's throats. Maybe if he kept doing it, she'd warm up to the grumpy Alpha in time. Abandoned childhood dreams be damned, I still believed there were few wounds that couldn't be healed by tea and time.

"You deserved the pillow to the face, and you know it," Arya said, pulling it back from my arms to hold it in her lap, "Now seriously, what the hell happened while you were gone?"

"I've already told you what happened." I shook my head. "I went because I wanted to know why Faye was about to blow her cover, I found her in the woods, Rory followed me there, and then Faye's girlfriend Nova turned Theo back into a man because apparently he wasn't dead, just cursed to live as if he were dead for all eternity."

The lesson of which was never fuck with a witch, or at least don't fuck a witch and forget to call the next day. He'd more than learned the error of his ways after that experience.

"Not what I'm asking about," she growled, "Don't make me throw another pillow at you."

"I don't know what else you could mean." Lies. I absolutely knew.

"Are you in a love triangle with an Alpha and a ghost, or

what?" Arya speared me with a look that was three parts 'tell me now' and two parts 'or else.'

"Of course not." One of them didn't seem to want me, and the other only wanted the memory he had of me.

"You can't tell me Rory didn't make a move on you before you left," she scoffed, "I'm honestly surprised he let you come home. The way he looked at you in the bar was so intense I almost expected him to lay a claiming bite on you then and there."

The growl in my chest came directly from my wolf. She'd softened slightly toward Rory after his confession. I think the knowledge that his wolf had planned to claim her as much as she'd once intended to claim him had soothed some of the animosity towards them, but she was far from ready to entertain talks of claiming.

"He said he'd be seeing me," I admitted, "But I have no plans of returning to Thornbridge territory anytime soon. It was like walking around and having a million pairs of eyes on me just waiting to see if I was going to slash them with my claws. As if I'd ever attack someone unprovoked."

"I'm kind of sad no one provoked you." Arya sighed wistfully, "You deserve to sharpen your claws on a few of those fools."

"Speaking of sharpening claws," I sat up straighter, "What's this I hear about you raking yours across a table at Howl?"

Beck had made a comment to her about watching her claws around tables as he'd left and a scarlet flush had spread across her cheeks. "What exactly were you and Beck doing that resulted in claw marks?"

"You know, I can't say I recall." The squeak of her voice told me otherwise. She drained her mug before holding the empty vessel out to me and asking, "Do you think you could get me some more tea? I'm kind of thirsty."

"I just bet you are," I said sweetly, but took the mug and climbed off the bed. A thud came from the wall as I walked through the door, and I suspected when I returned there'd be a pillow on the floor. Her aim wasn't nearly as good when her target was across the room.

I made my way down the stairs, through the living room and into the kitchen, pausing to give Skye a few belly rubs from her spot curled on the couch. She was resting on a pile of blankets I hadn't put there for her, and my heart melted a little that a certain man obviously had.

Something else of mine melted even more when I walked through the kitchen to see him leaning against the counter sipping a cup of his own tea in charcoal sweatpants and a white tee shirt that stood in stark contrast to his golden skin. It was the perfect level of tightness to show off the flex of his bicep as he raised the mug to his pillowy lips, not to mention the view of his forearms.

"You all right there?" he asked over the rim of his mug. Great. Just days after he sends me off into another man's arms, and I'm caught ogling him for the second time. When he walked out of the hall, hair still dripping onto that white tee shirt, I thought my heart may beat out of my chest. I thought Theo'd been handsome when he was still a ghost, but that was nothing compared to his appeal as a living man.

"I'm fine," I said after clearing my throat, "I'm just grabbing another mug of tea for Arya."

"I've got it." He set his own mug down before crossing the space between us to pluck ours from my hands. His fingers brushed over mine with the lightest touch, and I had to fight not to shiver as I met his ocean blue eyes.

"Thanks." I dropped his gaze and opted to take a seat on the counter while he set to boiling the kettle and grabbing another tea bag from the cupboard.

"So," I drew out while we waited for the water to come to temperature, "How does it feel being human again?"

It had to be at least a little overwhelming. If I was a better friend I would've already asked him this instead of focusing on my own woes. He was entering a world with nothing, and no one, and I'd only been thinking about if he would leave me now that he had the option. He'd had no choice but to stay before. I should be happy he was no longer a prisoner. If I was a better person I would set him free.

But I really, really didn't want to be a better person.

"It's colder," he said, cocking his head to one side then adding, "But there are positives to it too, I guess. Being able to smell, taste, and touch definitely has its perks."

"I imagine they do."

"For instance," he began and took one, then two steps toward me, "Did you know you smell like wildflowers and honey when you're happy, but the honey smells almost burnt when you're sad?"

I did know that. Rory had pointed it out to me once when we were teenagers, but I hadn't expected Theo to pick up on the subtleties of my scent. Warlocks didn't have the same sense of smell that shifters had. He walked closer until his hips were nearly touching my knees.

"And I think we both know which one I'm picking up on now." I looked down at my lap, my hair shifting forward as I did. "Why don't you tell me what's making you so sad, darling. Maybe I can fix it for you."

A warm hand brushed against my cheek as he tucked the curtain of hair that had fallen behind my ear.

"I'm going to miss you," I admitted softly. Theo dropped his hand.

"Miss me?" he asked. The step he took back felt like a mile between us. "I didn't realize either of us were going anywhere."

"Oh come on, Theo. We both know that as wonderful as it is that your curse is broken—really, it is—we can't exactly carry on the way we were."

"No?"

"You're not stuck here anymore," I said, the words bitter on my tongue, "You can go anywhere you want, do whatever you want, with whomever you want now! I don't expect you to stay here with me just because you feel like you have to."

"Willow that's not—"

"And if you did, what would that even look like?" I carried on, "We'd be roommates? I'd introduce myself to whoever you eventually brought home to meet the woman whose house you used to haunt, and you'd have a beer on the weekends with whatever male I end up mating and having a few pups with?"

The more I pictured it, the more sure I was that a life on the periphery of the other, but never fully together would be a sweet kind of torture I wouldn't be able to endure.

"And that's what you want?" Theo asked carefully, eyes searching every inch of my face, "For me to go find a life outside of you while you find a nice shifter to settle down with?"

No. Not even a little bit.

But what could I say to him that would keep him from giving me what I wanted out of obligation? What could I say that would set him free without lying to both him and myself?

As the kettle began to whistle, there was only one answer that entered my mind.

"I want you to be happy."

And if his happiness led me to my own unhappiness, I would have to learn to be okay with that. After all, how many people actually found their happily ever afters in the exact way they wanted to find it?

"Willow—"

I'd never know what it was that Theo was going to say, because at that moment a flash of headlights poured through our front windows, the beams reaching the kitchen through the open doorway.

"Um, not to alarm you this late at night," Arya called down from the top of the stairs, "But a truck just pulled up in your driveway and there's a guy getting out."

"I guess your Alpha couldn't stay away," Theo said tightly.

"He isn't—"

"You shouldn't keep him waiting." And with that he turned to take the kettle off the stove, poured the water into the tea bag-clad mug, and walked out of the kitchen. He didn't look at me once as he made his exit, leaving me to wonder if either of us were happy with this new arrangement at all.

CHAPTER 21

Theo

I want you to be happy.

Six words I'd never wanted to go back in time and un-say more than the moment they were thrown in my own face.

Listening to Willow in the kitchen had me questioning if we'd ever been on the same page at all. I thought she'd known, surely she'd *had to know* that if I'd thought there was a split second of a chance of walking this earth again, I would've never encouraged her to explore what could be between her and Rory.

Except obviously she hadn't. Which is how I found myself sitting across the kitchen table from the Alpha himself as we ate breakfast in silence alongside Willow and WD.

I'd seen Arya look nervously between the three of us more than once in the time we'd all been awake, only for Willow to shake her head at her friend without comment. But what did the shake of the head mean? What silent language existed between the two best friends, and when had my own silent language with Willow disappeared?

"So," I said, putting an end to the quiet meal, "Rory. You felt like the best time to take a trip to another pack's territory was just days after you removed its Beta from power? Your pack mates must be feeling very secure in their leadership these days."

Willow's elbow jabbed me in the ribs, but I didn't give Rory the satisfaction of seeing me flinch at her unspoken censure.

"They're fine," the wolf said without blinking.

"I love how your kind think whoever can win a staring contest is the stronger person of the two," I told Willow, "Like does he think staring at me will make me go away?"

"He can hear you as well as see you," she reminded me dryly.

"Oh darn, I guess I forgot." I shrugged innocently and turned back to Rory. "Ghostly habits die hard, and all that."

"I don't have to explain the decisions I make for my pack to you," he said. I'm sure he meant his tone to sound threatening, but I'd crossed a witch, walked amongst the dead, and come out the other side. What more did I really have to fear? Plus, as much as I'm sure he'd love to rake me through with his claws, regardless of the romantic feelings Willow may or may not have for him, she wouldn't take kindly to him scarring my pretty face.

"And I'm sure that's the attitude that had him missing out on eight years of your glorious presence with a piece of trash Beta at his side."

Willow's face planted into her hands. The words "For the love of god, Theo," managed to escape from between her fingers.

"Whoops." I snapped my fingers and pointed a finger at her, "Did it again, didn't I? You'll have to excuse me, I'm out of practice with my manners. I suppose the polite thing to do would be to sit here and pretend you hadn't royally fucked over Willow and Faye. My bad. I'll sit silently now to properly conform."

The guilt-stricken expression that overtook his face would've been far more satisfying if not for the slamming of hands against the table that came from beside me. All smugness left me, and I swore when I looked at Willow her eyes had a tinge of orange in them, dancing with flames of fury that would scald even the toughest of skin.

"Are you kidding me?" She didn't yell. Her voice was little more than a whisper. "Now you want to judge him?"

"Willow—"

"No," she shook her head and gave a chuckle that was too similar to a snarl for my comfort, "What did you tell me at the cottage? That Rory's a good man? My best chance at happiness?"

"I mean, technically yes, I did say that." And I was woefully regretting every syllable I'd uttered.

"Well forgive me if I've misinterpreted." Shit, she flipped her hair out of her face. She always meant business when her hair got flipped out of her face. "But you don't sound like someone who thinks he's a good man, so which is it? Were you lying then or are you lying now, because honestly, I'm not sure I can believe a single word leaving your mouth these days, maybe I never could."

"Low, maybe we should just—"

"Shut up, Rory, I'm still speaking."

He showed more wisdom than me when he complied. Willow took a deep breath and released it before continuing.

"Will you please," she drew out the final word, "just back off?"

"If that's what you want." The words were like sandpaper leaving my mouth. Willow didn't answer for a second, and I thought maybe, just for a minute, she'd say it wasn't. I thought maybe she would call me on my shit and tell me to fuck right off for trying to push her toward someone else. Because what kind of asshole was I that I could know what's best for her better than she would herself?

She'd tell me that we both knew this had nothing to do with the Alpha wolf, that it had never had anything to do with him in the first place. She'd tell me that both of us were being stupid. A miracle had been dropped into our laps, and we'd spent too much time already wasting it. I would tell her she was right, and then we'd be okay.

Except that isn't what she said.

Instead, the words that left her mouth were, "Yes, that is what I want."

And I watched the chance of a lifetime slip between my fingers as she rose from the table, said goodbye to Arya, and left. She took my heart and Rory with her.

CHAPTER 22

Willow

"Here you go."

I thanked Rory and brought the steaming mug of liquid happiness to my lips. I'd stormed out of the kitchen, thrown on whatever shoes and coat my fingers grabbed by the door, and walked to Rory's truck with little thought other than getting out of there. Which meant, of course, that I hadn't finished my coffee or thought to bring it with me when I left.

"So are we going to talk about it?" Rory asked as he slid into the seat across from mine.

"Talk about what?" Rory's indulgent smile should've warmed my heart, but it didn't.

"I'll take that as a no, then." He took a drink of his own coffee—black, of course—and said instead, "Then let's pretend it's just you and me here for a while instead."

I looked around the nearly empty cafe that was decked to the nines in hearts, lace, and garlands for the holiday. There was only one other patron in the corner typing away on her laptop, headphones covering her ears, and the barista who had served us. It was Valentine's Day, and I was feeling anything but warm and fuzzy.

"I don't think we'll need to pretend much," I pointed out, "I doubt anyone else here is paying us much attention."

"Not my meaning," came his response. He looked down at his mug then back up at me, "Tell me, when you left Thornbridge, why didn't you go to one of our rivals and join their ranks?"

Not what I had expected to come out of his mouth.

"What do you mean?"

"You were training to be an Enforcer," Rory said. He crossed his arms on the table in front of him and leaned forward toward me. "You could've surely gone to one of the larger packs, vied for a place in their ranks, and found no shortage of success. Instead you came to the Sun Meadow Pack. I mean no insult to Beck when I say this, but it's not exactly known for its strength."

"No," I laughed, "It's not. It's more like a pack of strays who found their way to the same area."

That was part of why I loved it. If he'd wanted to, I had no doubt Beckett could've built a pack that would rival the strength of any other. Though he kept it under wraps, I had my suspicions his dominance could even go against someone like Rory, but that wasn't what he did. Instead, he created a safe haven of community where we took care of one another. He and his ranked wolves kept order and peace, but I never felt like their will was being imposed on the rest of us.

"Exactly," Rory said, "So why come here instead?"

It took me a moment to gather the right words for my answer before speaking.

"Going to another pack would've been a betrayal," I admitted, "Even right after I left, I couldn't bring myself to do it. I never even considered it, if I'm being honest. If I'd joined the Briarwood Pack or even the Arrowroot Pack and you'd seen me at the next council meeting, I feel like that would've been the final nail in my coffin, you know?"

"You didn't want to shut the door completely."

I nodded.

If someone had asked me, I doubt I'd have admitted it aloud, but the idea of never being able to return if I wished it had been terrifying in the early days. Even though I was sure I'd never step foot back on pack lands, I wanted that to be my choice, not a choice that was taken from me. Becoming a ranked wolf somewhere else would've meant giving up that chance completely.

"And how do you feel now?" Rory's stare never wavered. "Do you want that door to be open?"

I should, shouldn't I? It could be so easy to fall back into old patterns. I could pack my bags, grab Skye, and run back to Thornbridge with Rory. I could stand at his side, help guide the pack, and make sure no one in its ranks would abuse their power ever again. I could smile as I walked by former friends turned foes and let them all see that I was the one who won in the end. I was the one who came out ahead. I could move into that beautiful white house and rock my pups on its wraparound porch next to an Alpha who looked at me with adoration. I could do all of that, if I wanted.

The problem was, I didn't.

"I'm very glad that you and I were able to reconcile," I said honestly and reached out to place a hand over his arm. My wolf tolerated the contact. Quite gracious of her.

"But you don't want to come back with me," he said with a certainty that held no malice or frustration, "Do you?"

"No." A ball of emotion sat in my throat at the admission. "I'm sorry, I don't."

Rory lifted his hand to place on top of mine and gave it a small squeeze.

"You don't need to apologize for not wanting to leave the home my mistakes drove you to build."

And damn if that didn't just about kill me.

"What happened in the kitchen this morning, Low?" he asked gently, his thumb ran soothingly along the back of my hand.

"Theo was being an asshole."

"Forgive me if I'm wrong, but based on your past depictions of him, I'm not sure that's anything new." Rory chuckled and shook his head. "And as far as I can tell, you usually kind of like it."

"Well today I didn't," came my very mature, very adult answer. What else could I say? The ghost I'd fallen in love with was giving me emotional whiplash and I was taking out my own disappointed heart on him and everyone around us?

"Okay," Rory drew out the word before trying a different angle, "Why do you think that is?"

"God, Rory what is this, twenty questions?" I groaned in frustration, "What are you trying to get at here?"

"I'm trying to keep you from making the same mistake that I made once, because whether you're coming home with me today or not, I care about you, Willow. I want you to be happy."

"You have no idea how tired I am of men telling me they just want me to be happy," both my wolf and growled, "Who are any of you to tell me what to want anyway?"

"Then why don't you tell me? What is it that you want?"

I wanted to go to my shift at the bar every night and joke around with the regulars while Arya and Beck tried not to tear each other's heads—or clothes—off. I wanted to wake up and have coffee on the porch with Skye while the sun rose. I wanted to come home, throw on an atrocious pair of fuzzy pajama pants and sit by the fire while the kettle boiled for a cup of tea.

I wanted someone to be there, beside me, enjoying all of those little things each day as much as I did.

And more than anything, I wanted that person to be Theo. I owed it both to him and to myself to find out for certain if he could want that too.

"Willow?" Rory asked, "Do you know what you want?"

"Yes. Yes, I do."

Rory's hand fell away from mine as he leaned back in his chair. He pointed over his shoulder and said, "Then you may want to run that direction, because I'm pretty sure *who* you want just passed by the window. I'd wager a pretty penny he glanced in here and didn't like what he saw."

My heart dropped to my stomach as I scrambled from my seat, knocking over one of the tiny heart candles on the table as I did. Thankfully they were the kind with fake flames.

I rushed toward the door but came to a halt, having enough courtesy to at least turn back to Rory and say, "Thank you."

"Go!" he urged, "Before he's too far to catch and you have to track him across town."

"Goodbye, Rory," I said and yanked open the door to embrace the chilled February air.

"Goodbye, Willow."

CHAPTER 23

Theo

I was too late.

I shouldn't have followed them. I knew I shouldn't have followed them, that it was only asking for trouble, but Arya's stupid ideas had been running through my head since she spoke to me in the kitchen.

"So your post-resurrection plan is just to watch your girl ride off into the sunset with someone else?" she'd asked after the door had shut behind Willow and Rory.

"I mean technically it's closer to sunrise," I'd pointed out in return. The little wolf looked far less than impressed with my witty retort. Instead she crossed her arms over her chest, leaned back in her chair, and gave me a stare down worthy of an Alpha.

"Are you secretly this pack's Luna?" I'd asked, only to earn an eye roll in return.

"Don't be ridiculous, Sable would wipe the floor with

me in a challenge any day of the week." She sounded certain but I wasn't so sure. "And don't try to change the subject; you're as bad as Willow with that."

"You were talking about sunsets, I brought up sunrises, and then you got a little cranky with me," I recapped, "I think the conversation was flowing rather nicely before your mood swing."

"I'm starting to see why that witch cursed you."

"Rude." It was too soon to joke about such things, even for me. "And I really don't think you're one to judge when it comes to messy exes."

A tinge of pink topped her cheeks as she huffed and said, "Don't mock me when I'm trying to help you."

"How is this helping me?" Because as far as I'd been able to tell, Willow was still angry with me, she and Rory had still gone off on whatever journey of reconnection they were on in the wee hours of the morning, and all that had changed from the moment they left until now was another wolf shifter getting angry with me for reasons I didn't even know.

"I'm telling you to go after her, you idiot!" Arya threw her hands in the air and practically yelled, "You literally have a second chance at life, why are you sitting here wasting it?"

"Willow's entitled to make her own choices." The words were bitter on my tongue. "If she wants to ride off into the sunrise with a half-decent Alpha in his truck, then that's entirely her call."

And if he was who she wanted, I'd just have to find a way to live with that.

"The funny thing about respecting people's choices is, we still need to give them the information to make them," Arya had said as she'd risen from her chair to go. "I'd hate for either of you to lose out on something wonderful because neither of you thought to give the other the courtesy of being honest. It's like you're a walking miscommunication trope, and I hate that shit. You can't choose something you don't know is an option, Theo."

"Message received, WD," I called after her, "I'll think about it." As if I'd thought of anything but Willow in years.

"Rory drove across two states to win back the woman he thinks he loves," Arya had said from the open front doorway, "With someone else being that proactive, you think about it too long, and you may just be too late."

She'd been right. I'd taken another twenty minutes before I'd rushed out of the house to go and find Willow. I thought I'd have to run into town or enchant Willow's car to take me, but Arya had been standing there, leaning against her SUV, waiting for me.

"Right choice." She'd lifted her keys and beeped the lock. "Get in."

I'd planned to go straight up to Willow, take her by the hand, pull her away from Rory, and tell her everything I'd wanted to say to her but hadn't. Except that isn't what happened. Because when I finally spotted Willow through that coffee shop window, her hand was on his arm, his hand was covering hers, and while I couldn't see the look on her face, I could see the look on his.

Complete contentment.

They'd reconciled.

She was happy, just not with me.

Now I was walking along the small downtown streets with no idea where I was heading other than away from the home I'd built but let crumble. How was I supposed to go back to the house and pretend watching them together didn't feel like a second death?

I'd have to leave.

I didn't know what I'd been thinking when I'd pushed her into his arms—even if I hadn't had that damned curse broken, I wouldn't have been able to stay and watch her build a life with anyone who wasn't me. I just had to keep it together for a few days. Just wait a little longer, and then the pack's contact would have my identification sorted out. Maybe Beck would help me look for a job. He was, after all, my best friend, and he kind of owed me one after the cold greeting he gave me my first night. I mean, what kind of bestie sees you for the first time and doesn't even give you a hug?

Yes. Beck would help.

I could do this. I could pretend everything was fine for a few more days, and during that time I would soak up every second I could with Willow that Rory wasn't around. I would ingrain her in every atom of my brain and body so when I left, she'd be as much a part of me as she was when I'd been at her side.

I would—

"Theo!" I turned toward the sound of Willow's voice behind me and watched as she ran toward me, raven black hair whipping in the wind. "Wait!"

For her?

Always.

CHAPTER 24

Willow

As my fur boot-clad feet pounded against the wet pavement I mentally added poor footwear choices to my list of mistakes this week. Every splash of water seemed to bloom against the shoes until each step I took had the squishy soles shooting icy water between my toes.

The things we endure for love.

I'd run up and down the streets of downtown searching for wherever Theo had wandered after he passed the shops, and hadn't seen a trace of him. I wasn't a fan of running in ideal conditions let alone in these. My lungs ached from the prolonged exertion. I really should've taken Arya up on the offer to join her morning jogs. Maybe then I wouldn't be huffing and puffing down main street darting past my wide-eyed pack mates.

Still, there was no sign of Theo. I couldn't have been more than a few minutes behind him, yet he was nowhere to be found. The man had been easier to locate when he was a ghost than he was as flesh and blood.

Where could he have gone? Surely, he wouldn't have left, not without at least saying goodbye, and not before we'd gotten his identification in order. His departure was beginning to look more and more likely when finally I turned the corner and saw a flash of golden blonde hair in the distance.

"Theo!" I screamed, social decorum and onlookers be damned, "Wait!"

His head whipped around until those ocean eyes met mine. Was it relief that crossed his face? God I hoped so. I hoped this was the moment where I found out we were both being idiots and had wanted to be together all along. I hoped this was the moment where happily ever after began, and there was no rug that was going to be pulled out from under me.

"Sorry!" I called to the mother pushing her stroller I barely avoided as I crossed the street.

Ten more steps and I was finally, finally coming to a halt in front of Theo. Unfortunately, the soles of my boots didn't get the memo that it was time to stop when they collided with a patch of ice. This time, when my feet flew out from under me, I didn't brace for impact or lament my once dry sweater as I careened toward the damp ground.

No. This time, I smiled because two warm arms wrapped themselves around my waist and lifted me upright.

"We really need to stop meeting like this," Theo said softly, his face hovering a few inches from mine, "It's going to give me a hero complex, and we both know I don't need the ego boost of acting like a savior."

"What can I say?" I asked breathlessly, half from the sprint to get here and half from how close his lips were to mine, "I guess I can't help myself from falling all over you."

A week ago we both would have smiled and laughed a comment like that off as nothing more than a joke. Today, neither of us were laughing. Theo's arms were firm as they pulled me up from my half-fallen position until we were both full upright again. My pack mates milled around us on the sidewalks, and I saw more than one eyebrow raise from the passersby.

The gossip mill would surely be churning that I was spotted with an unknown, attractive male on the street. The rumors would be extra juicy given my pajama-clad trip to visit Rory not a week prior, but I just couldn't bring myself to care.

The only thing I cared about then, in that exact moment, was the man standing in front of me, looking at me like he wasn't sure if I would be his salvation or his downfall.

"Where's Rory?" he asked, after he guided me off to the side of the walkway.

"I left him behind."

In more ways than one. I meant what I told Rory in the cafe. I was truly grateful to put the past pain between us to rest, and yet, I found myself eternally grateful for it. How could I be anything else?

"You two looked like you were having a nice conversation

when I happened by," Theo observed as he picked a non-existent piece of lint from his sleeve.

"We were." Under other circumstances I'd ask what he'd been doing at eight in the morning that he'd just 'happened by' where I was meeting with another man, but I refrained. There were more serious matters to discuss, and if they went the way I hoped, I'd circle back and tease him later.

"Then why didn't you stay with him?" he asked, his voice still guarded, but his eyes were beginning to soften.

"Why do you think?"

An airy chuckle left him as his mouth drew up at one corner, revealing that half-dimpled grin that made my legs feel wobbly. "I think I've made enough assumptions when it comes to you, and it hasn't helped either of us a single bit."

This was the moment, I realized as my heart raced faster in my chest and the palms of my hands began to feel the slightest bit sticky with sweat. I had to tell him. Even if he didn't feel the same way, or if he wanted to go explore the world now that he could truly be in it, we both deserved to lay our cards on the table.

I took a deep breath to steady myself and said, "I left him behind because when I think of my future, I can't imagine building it with anyone but you. Theo, I lo—"

The rest of my words were lost as Theo's hands grasped my face, fingers threading into my hair until they reached the base of my neck. Before I'd even taken my next breath, he anchored his mouth to mine. Sparks of electricity danced across my skin and ignited every cell, every instinct in my body.

My wolf howled in satisfaction as one word rang through my mind like a decree called down from the heavens.

Mate.

Theo was my mate.

Not just by choice, but by fate itself.

I could feel it in my bones, in my soul, that every piece of him was made for every piece of me. Tears welled behind my closed eyes as I wound my arms tightly around his neck and pressed against him until our bodies were flush.

"I love you too," he whispered against my lips.

"I didn't even get to fully say the words. I had a whole dramatically beautiful speech planned out, and you cut me off before I can get any of it out, let alone the most important parts."

Theo's smile grew and his forehead rested on mine as he asked, "Are you complaining? Should I take it back so you can start again?"

He moved as if to back away and I tightened my grip around his neck to hold him to me.

"I guess I can allow the interruption just this once." I said, tilting my chin up just a smidge. My lips brushed against his with each word. "Did you feel it?"

"I mean if you step a little closer, then I'm sure we both will." I couldn't see his grin but the gleam in his eye was positively devilish.

"Theodore!" I pulled the hair at the base of his neck and his eyes flared. I made a mental note of that for later. "Be serious for a moment."

"I am *always* serious when it comes to you," he teased. His eyes softened as he said, "Of course, I felt it, darling."

There wasn't an ounce of shock in his voice; it was pure, assured satisfaction.

"Did you know?" I drew my head back, not stepping out of his arms, but putting enough space between us that I could see his face.

"I didn't *know* per se," he shrugged, "but I may have suspected."

"Why didn't you ever say something?" If he had it would've saved us years of dancing around one another—or sent me into mourning thinking of a mate I could never hold. Maybe both.

"I couldn't be sure, and to be fair I did say I thought your mate had been cursed by a witch," he defended.

That he had. Fortunately for me, it turned out that a witch's curse was apparently more surmountable than being hit by a train.

I rose up on my sadly still squishy toes to place a peck against his lips and asked, "So does this mean you'll be my valentine?"

"This year and every year to come."

I couldn't think of anything better.

Theo dropped one of his arms from around my waist and let it drag along my torso and up my neck to brush a strand of hair behind my ear, leaving a trail of warmth in its wake.

I let my head rest in his open palm.

"You do know this means you have to haunt my every

step for all eternity, right?" Because there was no turning back now. I'd already come close to losing this before I even fully realized what I'd had. There was no chance of me letting him go now that I had.

"What do you think I've been doing all these years?" he asked smugly, "There's nowhere else I'd rather be than by your side, in your shadow—wherever and whenever you'll have me."

"Could you two try not to maul each other in public? There are children out and about." A deep voice tinged with annoyance called from across the street.

I looked over my shoulder to see a scowling Alpha shaking his head at us in disgust—or was it jealousy? Something told me if it were him and a certain wolf with cherry red hair he wouldn't be nearly as concerned about the two children out before school on a Friday.

"Sorry, Beck!" I yelled back with a little wave.

"Sorry, bestie!" Theo's cheeky grin looked anything but remorseful as Beck looked at him in horror before scurrying away. My mate turned his gaze back to me and cheerfully said, "I think he's warming up to me."

"Sure he is, love." Like an ice cube melting in a snowstorm. "He had a point though, we should probably move on from the sidewalk. We've attracted more than a few wagging tongues from the pack already. Soon someone will be brave enough to come interrogate us, and I'm not ready to share your attention with anyone else yet."

That and my feet really were freezing in those wet boots.

"You've had my full attention since the day we met, but I'm in no rush to divide it." He laced his fingers with mine, and asked, "Where should we go from here?"

I smiled.

"Home."

There was nothing better than having my mate wrapped in my arms under the stars, wearing my ring on her finger and my mark on her neck. I'd been hesitant to follow the shifter's custom of giving their mates a claiming bite. Willow had insisted it wasn't necessary and we could have our mating ceremony without the biting bit, but I could tell it was more important to her than she tried to let on.

Not to mention, I was all for anything that told others that every inch of her was mine. I stretched my head from side to side and smiled at the sting of my own punctured neck. I loved that I was marked as hers too.

"Today was perfect," my mate said dreamily as we swayed together on the outdoor dance floor, her head resting against my heart, arms wrapped tightly around my torso, long-sleeved white dress billowing around our feet. I did my best not to pick my feet up up for fear of damaging the lacy trim.

"Every day is perfect when I'm with you." My skin tingled where she giggled against me, but I meant every word I said. Willow was like my own personal sun. I'd happily orbit around her for the rest of my days, and pride swelled in my chest at the thought of being the person fate deemed worthy of being her mate.

"If you think about it," I pondered aloud, "It's actually a good thing that I hooked up with that witch. If I hadn't we may have never met."

"Can you not talk about sleeping with other women the night of our mating ceremony?" She groaned and looked up at me, her chin resting against the center of my chest. "It's killing my good mood."

"But at least it isn't killing *you*," I pointed out, "But I'll keep my musings to myself. Other women mean nothing to me, I'm just admiring the complicated sequence of events that led me to your door and thanking whatever entity that listens that they did."

She scrunched up her nose as her eyebrows drew in, "You have a unique kind of romanticism about you, you know that?"

"Glad you think so, darling." I brought my lips to her forehead before resting my chin atop her head, squeezing her to me.

It'd been ten months since the day we first said I love you, and every second was more amazing than I could've ever dreamed. Much to the dismay of the elders in the pack, I hadn't found my own place to live once it was clear I'd be staying in the pack. Some thought we were moving too fast by living together right away, but what they didn't fully understand was we'd been living together longer than they'd known I existed.

Other than those few naysayers, we'd received an overwhelming amount of support from the Sun Meadow Pack as we began our post-resurrection life together. Beck had been concerned some of the pack mates would *take issue* with a warlock on their territory, but it seemed their desire for Willow's happiness far outweighed any prejudices they may have held in the past.

As I glanced around the celebration over Willow's head, it looked like at least half the pack had even shown up to support us tonight in addition to a few out of town guests.

I wouldn't say we'd mended fences with Willow's parents since her trip back to the Thornbridge Pack, but we at least tried to be civil. According to Rory whose call I'd reluctantly watched Willow take, her mother had found the necklace where Willow left it and sobbed when Faye eventually made herself and Nova known to the pack a few months later.

For Willow's sake I was happy they'd reached out to try to reconcile, but I was far from ready to forgive them for their mistreatment of her. There was only so much you could say to try to atone for thinking your daughter killed her best friend, but Rory had assured Willow they were more than remorseful before she'd allowed them to contact her.

The Thornbridge Alpha had, unsurprisingly, declined our invitation to the ceremony, but sent a bottle of Willow's favorite wine to wish us well. I wasn't complaining about his absence. In fact, if he needed to keep his distance for the rest of our lives, that was a loss I was perfectly willing to bear.

My eyes continued their scan of our guests and landed on a trio I was happy to see getting along.

"It looks like Faye and Arya are becoming fast friends," I murmured to my mate. I felt the smile I could not see where her cheek rested against me.

"I'm not surprised, but I'm still glad to hear it," she said, "turn us so I can look and see without seeming like a creeper."

"Your wish is my command." We swayed back and forth in a small circle until the table we'd strategically put both of her closest friends at was in her direct line of sight.

"Nova looks bewildered," Willow giggled, "I can't say I blame her. Those two together will spell all sorts of trouble."

Even more so if my mate was thrown into the mix, but I chose to keep that observation to myself. No need to antagonize her on the day of our mating ceremony.

"Ugh," she groaned, turning rigid in my arms.

"What's wrong, darling?" Whatever the problem was I'd go fix it immediately. She deserved a perfect day and screw anyone who tried to impede on that perfection.

"I don't think Arya's date is quite as amused as Nova," she practically growled the words, "I don't know where she finds these men. Maybe we should interrupt."

The date in question had a sour look on his face as he watched the shifters and witch converse in their seats near one of the many outdoor heaters. So far it seemed like he'd stayed silent as he basked in whatever emotion plagued him, be it annoyance or frustration, but I doubted that would last much longer. What I was sure of, however, is that if I searched the crowd another pair of eyes would be tracking every move the couple made throughout the night.

"She does struggle when it comes to picking the right male, doesn't she?" I asked, knowing the answer. "It's a pity because when she isn't in WD mode, she's kind of the best."

"The best, huh?" Willow looked up at me with a raised brow and grin.

"After you of course." Obviously. As if Arya could hold a tea candle to her in my eyes.

"Of course." She settled back in against me. "I wish she could find her person, you know? She deserves that."

My eyes landed on Beck across the outdoor reception. "She does," I agreed. They both did.

As predicted his attention was laser focused on every move Arya and her date made, his stubble-covered jaw clenched tighter than an unopened jar of peanut butter.

"Yeah, I don't think her date's going to stay very long tonight," I surmised.

"Really?"

"In fact," I wagered, "I think he'll be heading out in three...two..."

The man yanked Arya's upper arm, and I winced as she flinched. Beck cut through the crowd like a knife and ripped the man from his seat. One hand wrapped around her date's neck as he brought his face within an inch of his snarling teeth.

"One."

Whatever Beck growled at the man had his face losing all color and Arya's mouth dropping open in shock. It was the first time I'd seen her speechless.

Beck tossed the man to the ground like a sack of flour and pointed to the exit. Seeing him intervene wasn't surprising. What did shock me, however, was what he did next.

Rather than angrily stalking off as the man scrambled away or turning his glower on Arya, he wrapped his arm around her waist, sat in the man's now vacant chair, and pulled her onto his lap until she was fully nestled against him.

"Things are about to get very interesting around here," Willow muttered. The smile in her voice was unmistakable.

"They definitely are," I agreed.

"They'd be so good together, don't you think? I feel like they'd balance each other out."

Or start world war three.

"Maybe we can double date," I suggested, "Beck and I need a new bonding activity now that I'm not enchanting the cleaning supplies at the bar anymore."

Stupid blocker runes. I should put a hex on whoever showed him how to place them. It was so much less efficient doing it by hand.

"I'll be sure to run that by him once we get back from our trip," she said dryly, "Unless you're planning to check in with him every day we're gone."

"No way." I pulled her tighter against me, loving the heat radiating from her body to mine. "I can't think of anything better than seven days of just you, me, a cozy cabin, and limited cell service."

She hummed her agreement and pulled back until I could see the contentment on her face. I swore she was more beautiful every time I looked at her.

"Neither can I." She raised up on her toes and I leaned down until her mouth was slanted beneath mine.

"I love you, Theo," she murmured against my lips.

"To the afterlife and back."

Also by Kathryn Covens

The Iolite Academy Series:

Forgotten Ashes

Abandoned Bonds (Coming 2025)

Acknowledgments

To Stephanie, for being the incredible alpha, beta, omega, & sanity-check-needed reader for everything I write! Thank you for listening to my daily updates, ideas, random, and often repetitive thoughts. I can't imagine doing this without you.

To my family, I love you! Thank you for seeing and supporting me as I go on this new journey.

To my Alpha Readers, Ashlee, Genna, and Stephanie thank you for taking time to read and share feedback on Ghosted by Love! Your thoughts and encouragement mean the world to me.

To my writing group, Alice, Brit, Genna, Wren, Vanessa, and Z, thank you for existing and pursuing this dream with me! I'm inspired by each and every one of you every day, and I am forever thankful to call you some of my best friends.

To my street team, you are simply the best! I have been blown away by the support you continue to show me and my writing. Thank you for everything you do!

To TGC, I love you more than cinnamon rolls. I hope you enjoyed the many TGC easter eggs in this book!

www.ingramcontent.com/pod-product-compliance
Lightning Source LLC
Chambersburg PA
CBHW032251310726
48973CB00008B/2378